Safe Colors

Thaddeus Rutkowski

Safe Colors

a novel in short fictions

COPYRIGHT © 2023 by Thaddeus Rutkowski

COVER ART by Shay Rutkowski
Bridge on East Houston Street (screen print)

AUTHOR PHOTO by Hollie Rutkowski

COVER AND BOOK DESIGN by Alexandru Oprescu

LIBRARY OF CONGRESS CATALOGING-IN-PUBLICATION DATA

Safe Colors: A Novel in Short Fictions
Authored by Thaddeus Rutkowski

ISBN: 9798985965971
LCCN: 2023935891

For
Randi Hoffman
and
Shay Rutkowski

contents

— PART TWO —

— PART THREE —

part one

Nowhere Boy

AN ELECTRIC RADIO SAT ON TOP OF THE REFRIGERATOR in my family's house. I never touched it—my mother was the one who turned the radio on. She liked music in the morning, and sometimes she would sing along.

The radio had a clockface that told my siblings and me when it was time to leave for school. Between seven and eight a.m., the radio played the hits through its monaural speaker. Out of all of those songs, the one that stuck in my mind was "Nowhere Man." The melody hooked me, but the lyrics didn't mean much. I certainly lived in a Nowhere Land—a small town in northern Appalachia—but was I a real Nowhere Man? Was I a man at all, or just a boy? I definitely felt like a boy. Did I have any Nowhere plans? I wanted to leave Nowhere and get Somewhere. Would I be able to do that, or would I go from Nowhere to Nowhere?

I knew where Somewhere was. It was in the shows I saw on television. Where I lived was not on television, and the people I saw on television didn't come to where I lived. That would have helped, if some TV actor showed up where I lived or where I went to school. That would have proved I was Someone. But I knew no TV actors. I was No One.

I didn't have high expectations for a change in my situation. I just wanted to get to school on time.

—

One morning, I heard my mother singing "Nowhere Man." She had most of the words right. When she stopped singing, she said, "It starts out well; then it repeats. But it doesn't go crazy, like most of the songs I hear."

Listening to her made me late. I slammed out the door and ran for the school bus.

—

In physical-education class, I jogged with the rest of the boys around a dirt track. As we high-stepped, we chanted, "From the halls of Montezuma to the shores of Tripoli …"

Our gym instructor jogged along with us. "You'll be ready for the Marines when you leave here," he said. "But when you get to boot camp, you'll have to sing in a room filled with tear gas."

I wondered if we would have to jog in place in the gas room, or whether we could sit in a chair while we wept and sang.

We rounded the first turn in the track. As we pumped our arms and lifted our knees, we called out: "We fight our country's battles in the air, on land, and sea."

"You'll put on a gas mask," the instructor continued. "Then you'll take the mask off and keep singing. If you can't do it, you'll start again. You'll repeat until you get through the song. When you're done, you'll pass one test for the Marines."

As we neared the finish line, we shouted, "We have fought in every clime and place where we could take a gun!"

"Run, Sweet Peas!" the instructor yelled.

I collapsed as I crossed the end line. I wasn't able to join in on the coda.

~

My mother asked if she should buy a violin. "I saw an ad in the paper for a used one," she said.

"Who is it for?" I asked.

"For me," she said.

"How would you learn to play it?"

"I'll follow my ear. I listened to the Chinese violin when I was a child. It has two strings, and this has four."

"Won't you need lessons?"

"I can hear the notes in my head."

"You should use the money for something else," I said.

Presently, my mother bought the violin. It rested in a velvet-lined case and was made of red-brown wood. When my mother drew the bow over the strings, the sound box gave out a loud, rich drone. "It sounds like the Chinese *erhu*," she said.

She played a few notes that didn't follow any recognizable pattern, then put the violin away.

Later, I opened the case, unclipped the bow, picked up the instrument, and drew the bow across a string. My skull vibrated in sympathy with the sound.

~

An artist friend of my father's came from New York City to visit.

At one point, my father asked him, "Do you ever see any celebrities there?"

"I was at a party with George Harrison," the friend said.

When I heard this, I knew the friend had been carousing with the Nowhere Man himself, or at least with one of the musicians on the song. Harrison was a Somewhere Man. He got Somewhere by heeding his own advice about living in Nowhere. He made his plans for Somewhere and left.

My father's friend was an ambassador from Someplace. I believed he could help me do Something.

"Did you talk to George?" I asked.

"No. That would be the thing *not* to do."

I could imagine the Somewhere people milling around with drinks in their hands, talking to who they were supposed to talk to, making sure they stayed Someplace, making certain they didn't return to Nowhere.

⁓

In chorus practice in school, our teacher played the piano while we sang. The teacher liked songs with a message—with a conscience—so she told us to open our music books to "Blowin' in the Wind." As she played the intro, we came in with the words.

I was a bad singer—I had trouble carrying a tune, even when the teacher played it slowly. So I repeated what the boys around me sang. Unfortunately, the boys hated the song. Instead of singing the line "The answer is blowin' in the wind," they chanted, "The answer is *blow me* in the wind."

⁓

In the morning, I heard my mother playing "You Are My Sunshine" on her violin. All of the notes were right; I recognized the song.

"How did you learn that?" I asked.

"I sang it in my head; then I played it."

"Can you play 'Nowhere Man'?"

"Let's see."

She scraped out the first few notes on her violin. The sequence sounded familiar. She was translating the melody to the instrument. She would have to spend some time practicing, but soon she would bring the song home.

Changeups

AT THE BEGINNING OF THE SCHOOL YEAR, A TEACHER looked at his roster, then stared at me and asked, "What is your name?"

I told him, and he looked back at his roster. "Can you spell it?" he asked.

I spelled my name.

"Your first name is different here," he said.

"I use my middle name as my first name," I said.

"Why is that?"

"It's what I've always been called."

"What about your last name?"

"It's my father's name, but I've thought about using my mother's name."

The teacher motioned for me to move forward. "You can sit in the first row, in the seat of honor," he said.

After class, a student repeated in a mocking tone, " 'I've thought about using my mother's name.' "

⁓

After school, I went to a stream that ran through a field near my family's house. I followed a dirt lane through a loose dog's territory. I faced the dog down, and it didn't bite me.

I walked along the stream, stepping over puddles formed by a recent rain, until I came to a large shallow pool. Many sulfur butterflies hovered there, forming a yellow cloud over the water. In the field, thistles were in bloom, and orange fritillaries clustered around the purple blossoms.

A boy was fishing with bait threaded onto a hook. He whipped his rod, and somehow the hook caught his free hand. I walked up to him and saw that he'd pierced his own finger. The metal point entered in one spot, curved through the flesh, and reemerged. The hook couldn't be pulled out; the barb wouldn't allow it to go back through the skin.

"You should see a doctor," I said.

⁓

When I got home, my father called me to his studio. The small room was musty and hot. He rolled a cigarette over his drawing table, drank from a beer bottle, and said, "Don't be an artist."

I stood in the doorway—I couldn't leave until I was dismissed. There was a sill on the floor below the doorframe, and my feet wouldn't balance.

"Don't pick up a pencil or brush," he continued.

He pointed to a charcoal drawing tacked to the wall. Curved lines radiated from the center, making a pattern like a target of arcs. The lines were smooth and perfect. "Do you know what it is?" he asked.

I shrugged as my feet teetered on the crosspiece.

"Is it good?"

I nodded and steadied myself with a hand on the doorframe.

"How can you know if it's good if you don't know what it is?" he shouted.

He stared at the surface of his table as his hand-rolled cigarette crumbled into ash. "It's a weeping willow," he said. "The black lines are branches. They bend with the weight of the tree's tears."

I couldn't see it.

"You're dismissed."

—

When my mother got home from her job at the county hospital, she said, "A boy came in with a hook through his finger."

"I saw him fishing," I said.

"They had to use wire clippers to get the hook out. They cut the shaft, and the pieces slid free."

—

I tried to draw lines in perfect arcs, like those in my father's drawing. I found a large sheet of paper and some sticks of charcoal and set the paper on the floor. However, I couldn't find a compass with a large enough radius to draw lines like those I'd seen. I took a nail and tied a string around it, then hammered the nail into the floor. I was sure other people in the house could hear the pounding; my room was next to my brother and sister's room. But my door was shut, as was theirs. No one came to question me.

I taped a piece of charcoal to the end of the string and produced a large black arc. I pulled up the nail with the hammer's claw and sank it in a different place, then drew another line. I repeated this process until I had a network of curved lines. I also had made a number of holes in the floor. My drawing looked nothing like the tendrils of a willow, but the lines were clear and strong.

~

In school, I went to my seat at the front of the room. Students sitting behind me could see only the back of my head. I heard a boy ask, "Where's he from?"

"The tropics," someone said.

"Jap," someone else said.

I wasn't from Japan, and no one in my family was from there, but I didn't say anything. I didn't want to explain that my mother's father had come to the United States from China to study at a seminary, and my mother had followed sometime later.

When the teacher arrived, he said to me, "You're sitting in your new seat. What's your name again?"

"I'm thinking of changing it to my mother's name, Wong."

"OK, Mr. Wong."

~

At home, I brought my charcoal drawing to my father's studio. The room was empty, so I looked briefly at the drawings on the wall. One showed a cicada larva, magnified many times. The insect had burst from the ground and was floating in space. It was going to attach itself to a tree or a building and metamorphose into the largest flying creature ever seen. The only color used was black—applied with a paintbrush in thick, exact strokes.

I rolled up my drawing and set it in a corner of the room, where my father might find it later.

Iced

I WOKE AND SAW THAT ICE CRYSTALS HAD FORMED ON THE inside of my bedroom window. The crystals lay in an intricate branching pattern that started at the bottom of the pane and grew over the glass. A complex system was at work. But I didn't care about the atomic order of the dendritic shapes; I wanted to mess up the ice.

I drew a fingernail over the ice to make clear lines; I held the balls of my fingers against the coating to make holes. The scene outside came into view: interrupted telephone wires, black trees, a paved street. I could see, on the other side of the street, a house that had no door, just a wooden frame with plastic over it. A family lived there; I knew the children: one was a girl.

My father took my siblings and me to a frozen lake that lay between mountains. He led us to a random site on the lake, where he took out a hatchet. He hacked at the ice until he had made a hole about a foot wide. "We camped on the ice when I was in the Army," he said. "We were getting ready for the Russian front."

My father set up a rig with a line and reel, baited a hook, and dropped it through the hole. He bent a flag on a wire and fastened it. We stood around waiting for the flag to spring.

Presently, the sun came out. "Fish feed when the air gets warmer," my father said. "They start moving."

I pictured fish circling in the frigid water below our rig, coming toward the light to search for food.

―

At home, my mother asked, "Did you catch anything?"

"No luck," my father said.

"Where I grew up, carp lived in the rice paddies," my mother replied. "You didn't need a hook and bait. You could catch the fish with your hands. Boys would hold the carp like babies."

"Here," my father said, "if you're camping and you catch a carp, you cook it on a board over a fire. You throw away the fish and eat the board."

―

Later, my father called me to his studio and said, "I'm going to make a painting of ice. I'm going to use the white canvas as positive space. Over it, I'll put a thin line—the horizon. Above that, a gray sky."

He picked up a blank canvas and set it on an easel.

I stood in the doorway and looked at the floor.

"It's up to you to amuse yourself," he said. "I can't do it. Take your brother and sister and go for a walk. Take a shovel. If the pond is frozen, clear it off and skate on it."

I did as I was told. When my brother and sister and I reached the nearby pond, we used a wide shovel to make random paths through the covering of snow. The ice was rough—the result of melting and freezing again. We put on our skates and slid around. The bumps in the ice made our feet rumble.

⌐

When we got home, I saw the girl from the house across the street leaving my father's studio. We recognized each other but didn't speak.

My father came out of the room and said, "She's not like my own kids. She understands what I'm doing. I'm going to invite her again."

⌐

I picked up a small shovel—a spade my father kept from his time in the Army—and walked on a path out of town. Presently, I came to a depression between hills. Long ago, a body of salt water filled the basin. A Devonian sea covered central Pennsylvania.

I began to dig. I had the idea that the snow and ice could have dislodged something—an animal carcass or, better yet, a human corpse—then frozen around it. The snow could have hidden anything. Perhaps the "missing link" was buried here. No hoax was involved. I was looking for the real thing: a creature that was half human, half ape.

I kept moving snow but found nothing. In time, I reached a piece of red fabric. Maybe this was a burial shroud. Maybe I was solving an age-old mystery. But the scrap turned out to be a discarded piece of clothing. It looked like a jacket belonging to a child.

⌐

When I got home, my father saw the spade and asked, "What were you doing? Digging a foxhole? You'll need to dig deep when you get to the Russian front. You'll need to keep from freezing to death."

When my mother saw the spade, she said, "I've been shoveling snow all day. My joints hurt. I can barely make it up the stairs. So I just walk slowly."

I put the spade back with my father's other Army souvenir: a Samurai sword. The spade and the sword shared a corner in his studio. I looked around and noticed that my father had started to make a painting of the girl who lived across the street. On the canvas, the girl was standing in the doorway of the house that had no door.

⌣

Later, my father fired up the coal furnace that heated our house. Hot water rose through exposed copper pipes and filled the radiators. The ice crystals on my window melted away.

During the night, I dreamed that I was passing over a large area of mountains. Snow covered the peaks: These were relatively young, jagged mountains. The unfriendly terrain went on for hundreds—maybe thousands—of miles, but I was traveling fast, close to the speed of sound. The icy rocks rolled out below me. The scene was uniform, beautiful, nonthreatening. I knew that, on the southern side of the harsh landscape, the climate would turn warmer. I would go from the Arctic to a temperate zone. Soon, I would be in the tropics.

Bad Chemistry

IN SCHOOL, MY BROTHER AND SISTER AND I TRIED OUT FOR roles in the student production of *South Pacific*. We didn't win major roles, but we were selected to play island dancers. Our part was to sing in the chorus and make simple moves in an ensemble. When we weren't performing, we would kneel on the stage. For costumes, we would wear loincloths—what the natives wore while they entertained U.S. servicemen. I was disappointed with my small part, but I was ready to go to rehearsals and perform in the play.

My father, however, became angry with this result. "My kids aren't going to be typecast!" he shouted. "They aren't Pacific Islanders!"

"I don't see what's wrong with it," my mother said. "They are half Chinese."

⁓

The next day, I told the teacher/director that we were quitting the production. "We aren't allowed to portray Asians," I explained.

"Where are you from?" the teacher asked.

"I'm from here," I said. "About ten miles away."

"I mean, where were you born?"

"I was born in this state."

"I mean, where are your parents from?"

"He's an Eskimo!" a boy in the class called out.

"Nanook!" someone else said.

⁓

My father took my siblings and me to see a movie. "Since you can't be in the musical, we'll see the only show in town," he said.

The movie told the story of a chemistry professor who had invented a new rubber-gas substance. The stuff caused all people, including the professor, to blow up like balloons. They floated through the air, and when they touched down they bounced. Otherwise, the plot was unclear. A marriage (the professor's) was breaking up, and another man was moving in on the separating wife. At the end of the movie, the professor's wife came back to him and a football filled with rubber gas bounced into outer space.

⁓

My father gave me some laboratory equipment: flasks, rubber stoppers, glass tubing, and an alcohol lamp. "I saved these from college," he said. "I didn't need them when I switched to art. You should do something useful with them."

I hooked up the parts on a table in my bedroom and boiled water in a flask. What I wanted to do was make poison. However, I had no toxic chemicals—no arsenic, lead, or potassium cyanide. All I had was what was in the house. I had the potassium found in bananas, and that certainly wasn't poisonous.

So I went outside and picked some nightshade berries. I crushed them in a test tube and added water to create a powerful alkaloid brew. I heated the mixture until it boiled. The stuff gave off a noxious smell that filled my room. I could kill with this red goo. But I didn't know who to kill.

My father came in and looked at my setup. "That smells like a mean soup," he said.

—

My father took me to the local bar and sat me on a stool beside him. He asked the bartender for a shot, and when he got it he swirled the bourbon in his mouth.

"Do you want another?" the bartender asked.

"Yes," my father said as he took out a small glass beaker. "But pour it in here. This is the size of a real shot; it's accurate to the milliliter."

My father poured the measured liquid into the bar's shot glass, and the bourbon spilled over. "Your glass has a false bottom," he said.

He tested several shot glasses from the bar, and all of them had false bottoms. My father rejected the bar's shots and drank from his beaker. "This is what you do with lab equipment," he said to me.

—

When my father lost his driver's license due to intoxication, my mother gave him rides, but she would not take him to the local bar.

"Let's go down the road," my father would say, "for a snifter."

"No," my mother would reply.

"Just one snifter."

"I don't think so."

"When I get my license back, the first place I'm going is the bar."

—

A Japanese friend of my mother's came to visit. She looked at me and said, "I can't see it."

"Can't see what?" my mother asked.

"The Asian side."

"It's there, but Asians can't see it."

"Now that you say it, I can see it—a little."

~

I decided to make something useful with my chemistry set. I had a small bottle of fluoride salts—the chemical sounded like an ingredient in toothpaste. With a mortar and pestle, I ground the powder with water and added sugar. I didn't want too much water; I didn't want the paste to run like soup. My mixture looked like the gunk sold in the dental-care aisle in drugstores, but it didn't smell the same. I put the goop into a heavy plastic bag and punched a hole in one end. When the bag was squeezed, the paste would ooze onto a toothbrush.

I showed my mother the product.

She didn't look long at the bag, and she didn't want to hear my sales pitch. "I don't use toothpaste," she said. "I use baking soda. Sodium bicarbonate fights germs.

"And I don't use floss," she added. "I use a straight pin."

~

When my father returned from his first trip back to the bar, he called me to his workroom. He said, "I used to think that silk-screened prints would sell. Paintings are expensive, but prints are cheap. I made prints of butterflies, but nobody bought them. So I have a better idea. I want to invent the next wheel, the next thing like a wheel. Something like a Hula-Hoop. No one would already have one, but everyone would want one. I'll get rich overnight."

~

I wanted to invent something that would explode, so I raided my father's stash of hunting ammunition. I sliced open some shotgun shells and poured out the powder.

I invited my brother and sister to watch my demonstration. I carefully packed the black grains into a glass tube held vertically on an armature. When I touched a match to the gunpowder, a flame shot toward the ceiling. My brother and sister started to laugh, but I didn't see the humor in what was happening.

The flame blossomed into an orange cloud that clung to the surface above. The nebulous fire spread quickly. The smell of saltpeter filled the air. I was terrified, but my siblings just kept laughing.

Unworldly Incidents

AS DAYLIGHT FADED, I HEARD MY MOTHER CALLING my name. She repeated the three syllables loudly, with an intonation, almost like a song. I wasn't far away, maybe a couple of hundred yards. I heard her voice and started to return home across neighbors' lawns.

As I passed one house, I looked in through the window and saw a lit television. There was a black-and-white pattern on the screen. The image was fluttering, stretching, dissolving while an announcer explained, "There is nothing wrong with your television set. ... We are controlling transmission."

My surroundings suddenly looked different, more frightening. I believed that aliens from space were controlling the television. Where were they from? The red planet? A red star? If they could make the picture on the tube go crazy, they could do the same with the world as I knew it. They could transport creatures with melted faces to Earth—to the back yard where I was standing.

I started to run. When I got home, I tuned our TV set to the frequency where aliens were directing transmission. I wanted to know what they were doing. I wanted to know before they did it. I wanted to be ready.

My father told me about a UFO that had landed nearby. "It was in the paper," he said. "It was just like that incident in New England. A man and woman were driving along a mountain road at night, and the ship landed in front of them."

"What did it look like?" I asked.

"Like an object, a flying object! The witnesses didn't specify. It was big."

"Did it fly away?"

"Of course it did, but before it did, it transported the woman inside, then released her."

I wondered why space creatures would arrive and fly away. "Maybe the 'aliens' were people," I said.

"They might have been people, but they were a different kind of people! They're going to replace regular people."

My father took me in his car to see the landing site. He parked on a narrow road between two hills. The trees on both sides of the road had been flattened.

We got out to examine the tree trunks. They had not been cut by logging saws—they were splintered near the base. A great force had knocked them down.

"Maybe it was a high wind," I said.

"It was a wind, all right," my father said. "It was the wind from a spaceship's engine. This is just the first step. Soon, the new people will wipe out the old people, and a new order will begin."

At my bedroom desk, I constructed a model rocket from balsa wood and cardboard. The rocket, according to the kit, was called the *Mars Snooper*. Its fins were large, with pods on the ends. The winglike fins would help the *Snooper* navigate the thin Martian atmosphere.

I painted the model rocket red, with gold trim. My lines were wobbly—my eye-hand control wasn't skilled.

When my father saw my paint job, he went over it with his own brush. His edges were perfectly straight. His hand was steady—a surprising quality, I thought, since he was under the influence of alcohol much of the time.

⌣

My father took my family out to test-fly the *Mars Snooper*. He drove to a hilltop where there were tree stumps, but no trees. He asked all of us to pose by the rocket launcher while he took a photograph. The *Snooper* sat on its large fins; my mother, brother, sister, and I stood behind it. My father opened the car hood and ran wires from the battery to the rocket engine. We stood still while he snapped his camera shutter.

Moments later, I pressed the launch button, and the *Snooper* shot up a long way—it must have reached a thousand feet before it lost energy, reversed direction and deployed its parachute. My siblings and I ran across the cleared ground to retrieve it.

⌣

On our way home, we saw a man in black walking beside the road. He was wearing a wide-brimmed hat, a long jacket, and pants that were too short. He had a thick beard, and there were no buttons on his clothes.

My father stopped to pick him up. I recognized him as one of our neighbors: an Amish man.

"There was a flying saucer!" my brother and sister said.

"Right," the man said. "It stopped at our farm, flattened a cornfield." When he spoke, he looked like he was in pain.

When my mother asked what was wrong, he said, "I had all of my teeth pulled."

"Who did it?" my mother asked.

"One of our dentists. He did it naturally—no medicine. I think he had help."

I pictured an Amish dentist in a black apron twisting each of the man's teeth out with a pair of pliers while his patient tried not to move or make a sound. I hoped the dentist had pulled each tooth quickly, with finesse.

"But I got a set of dentures," the man continued. "We're good at making dentures. They don't hurt yet."

"Don't worry," my father said, "when the new society comes, we'll be with them."

~

I turned on our television and found a show about space travel filmed in "Supermarionation." In it, marionettes named Steve Zodiac and Venus were piloting a rocket ship. Their craft looked something like my *Mars Snooper*. It had wide fins, almost like airplane wings.

Steve Zodiac and Venus thwarted any attempt by aliens to invade Earth. They stopped some of the Others from burning the planet, and still Others from freezing the ecosystem. The couple did these things, even though their movements were jerky and their jaws were not synced with their words. But what did I expect from Supermarionation?

~

My father took me to a friend's house on the top of a hill. The three of us went outside on a chilly night, one of the longest nights of the year. The two men had set up chairs so they could watch the skies. They were drinking beers—to keep warm, they said.

"We're waiting for UFOs," my father explained to me. "If they don't come, we'll at least see northern lights.

I walked around as they sat. All of us were waiting for flying objects, or at least dancing curtains, to appear in the sky.

We stayed out, and no UFOs or auroras arrived. But we did see some oddly behaving lights. The glowing spots were as bright as stars, and they moved quickly across our field of vision. That motion wasn't unusual; they could have been aircraft. Then one stopped, and another began to circle it. I wondered what kind of aircraft would do that. Helicopters? But these lights seemed far away, part of the firmament.

"They aren't stars or planets," my father said. "They're moving too fast."

"They're not meteors," his friend said. "They didn't burn up in the atmosphere."

After a while, the circling stopped and the two objects continued on parallel paths across the sky. My father and his friend continued to drink. I went inside.

Sights and Sounds

MY FATHER TOOK ME TO VISIT A NEW FRIEND OF HIS. "I met him at the bar," my father told me during the ride there. "He has his head on straight, not like the rest of the people around here."

The man lived in a small house next to a farm—the house had a tarpaper roof and imitation-wood shingles. When we got inside, my father and his friend had some drinks. Then the man took us down to his basement—a space with a low ceiling and a coal furnace. The only light came from an incandescent bulb hanging from a wire. The man led us to a corner sectioned off with wood planks. A large pig—a hog—stood in the enclosure with its hindquarters to us. The animal must have weighed a couple of hundred pounds. The pig couldn't walk around in its pen—its bulk filled the enclosure—but it could lie on straw on the cement floor.

I noticed there wasn't much of a smell. Either the straw had been changed recently, or this was a clean pig.

"What are you going to do with it?" my father asked.

"When it gets big enough, we'll show it at the county fair," the friend said. "This is a prize hog. It will win a ribbon."

⌣

In the evening, my father took my family to a classical-music concert at the state university. We rode in his car to an auditorium about twenty miles away. The auditorium was in a gymnasium—the stage was raised above the floor, and chairs were aligned on the basketball court.

The orchestra featured a harpist; she was the musician I focused on. She was wearing a long gown, and her shoulders were bare. I looked for her in the program, found her name, and tried to remember it.

The concert meant little to me. The music was pleasant enough, but the musicians didn't do anything except sit and play. The motion of the conductor's hands and arms didn't hold my interest. I couldn't tell what was coming next—I didn't know the musical score—but nothing new ever came next. It was always more of the same, just at a louder or softer volume.

⌣

The next day, I watched a parade with my brother and sister. There was a rise in our lawn next to the street, and the incline made a good seat. Trucks and emergency vehicles from nearby fire stations rolled by. On some of the vehicles were beauty queens, who waved as they passed. Between the fire engines, school bands with baton twirlers marched. The majorettes kicked up their skirts with their knees as they approached.

Near the end of the parade, I saw the hog from the basement we'd visited. The animal was riding in the back of a pickup truck, and my father's friend was driving. The hog still couldn't move around much, but it could look out over the sideboard. The man waved, and the hog made eye contact with me, as if it, too, remembered our meeting.

From another room, I could hear my father listening to music on his stereo system. I pictured him drinking beer and smoking tobacco. I was sure he didn't want to be disturbed.

After a while, he stopped playing records and walked out of the house. At that moment, I went for the stereo. The system had an amplifier powered by vacuum tubes, and when I turned the component on, I could see the tubes warming up in the metal box. In their hot state, the tubes glowed orange. The amplifier put out a lot of wattage, and the sound was powerful. Each speaker stood about three feet high. When I turned the volume knob past halfway, the sound was ear-splitting. That was the way I liked it.

I couldn't find any harp music; anyway, I didn't want classical music. So I shut the door and listened to rock music—the harder the better. I put on a British electric-guitar band. I knew my mother was in the next room, but I was rude.

When my mother came through the door, she didn't say anything.

I turned down the volume, and she stood there in her apron, looking at me. "When they sing, I can't understand the words," she said. "I can tell they're angry, but I don't know what they're angry about."

On the weekend, my father took my siblings and me to a hog-slaughtering party. When we arrived at a nearby farm, the killing had already taken place, but the butchering—the cutting and trimming—was still going on. A number of people filled the barn, where various animal parts were being prepared. There were slabs—steaks—and there was ground meat. I noticed three hogs' heads resting on a plank. They had been shot through the top of the skull. I guessed that was the quickest method of execution, humane in some way. I didn't see the face of the prize hog that belonged to my father's friend.

My brother and sister and I walked around, surrounded by potential food. The place didn't smell good at first—it smelled of blood and lard. Then I got used to the stench, and it started to smell good.

—

Late at night, I again heard my father listening to music—a piece I didn't recognize. I pictured him slowed from drink, his eyes half-closed. He would stay in this state for a long time, maybe all night. Then, not having slept, he would "get up" for the day.

I also couldn't sleep. I looked at the mechanical clock on the table next to my bed. I calculated the hours I would sleep, if I ever did fall asleep. The ticking clock showed eleven p.m. If I got up at six a.m., I would have seven hours of sleep. That would be enough; I would get through the school day without feeling tired. I listened to the music from downstairs. It had become louder—my father had switched to gospel blues sung by a woman.

My mother came into the room and saw that I was awake. "Some people slept all the time where I grew up," she said. "That's because they were smoking opium. They lived in dens and got very thin. You shouldn't try that."

I didn't want to try it, but nevertheless I couldn't relax. When I next looked at the clock, it was one a.m. That would leave me five hours of sleep. I started counting in my head, "One, two, three ..." The idea was to think about nothing.

But it was hard to focus on the numbers. How far had I gotten? Was I in the one hundreds or the two hundreds?

I couldn't remember. I was thinking about the baton twirlers in the parade and the harp player in the orchestra. I started counting again. In about an hour, I had reached one thousand. I was more wakeful than ever. I got out of bed and walked around my room, still counting in my head. I lay down again. The clock showed three in the morning. I kept counting.

Bird-Watching

MY FAMILY ACQUIRED A DUCKLING AT A LOCAL CARNIVAL. The bird was a prize in a game of chance. The way the game worked was, contestants threw Ping-Pong balls at small glass vases. Most times, the tossed ball would bounce off the lip of a vase and roll into a trough, where it would be redirected to the next player. On one throw, however, my brother hit a cup and won a duckling that was dyed blue.

The duckling appeared to be female—she had a wide chest and a relatively short neck. Over the next weeks, she grew fast, and all of her blue down fell out. The bird, who wasn't named, became her natural color—white—as feathers appeared. She also outgrew our living room, where she had been living on newspaper sheets spread on the floor. I didn't miss the newspaper nest; we already had two dogs that made the kitchen their home.

To accommodate the growing bird, my father built a coop in the yard. He made a duck house out of plywood, with vertical two-by-fours to keep it off the ground. The coop had a wire-mesh front so the bird could see out—and we could see in. My father scattered straw on the wire-mesh floor.

The duck seemed to thrive there. Sometimes we let her out so she could roam the yard, though someone had to watch her all the time. She clicked her beak as she walked, snapping at insects and reducing the pests. But her snapping action might have been a threat; she looked like she could deliver a strong pinch. When she came toward me with her beak clapping, I moved out of her way. I didn't want to get "goosed."

I remembered seeing an artist's illustration of a child herding ducks with a stick. The image was in a book of Mother Goose rhymes, though not all of the animals in the book were birds. The inclusion of ducks among the verses seemed coincidental; the only bird with a purpose was Mother Goose herself. She told the stories through rhymes.

In any case, the birds in the Mother Goose book were running away from a stick as the child held the weapon over their heads.

I tried the stick method with our duck. I picked up a branch and held it behind her head. She was frightened; she didn't want to be touched. With the stick in my hand, I was in no danger of being pinched. But I didn't know where we should go, she and I, so I "herded" her through random patterns in the yard.

Over the weeks, she laid eggs, and my father collected them. The eggs were larger than a hen's eggs, and the shells concealed a tough inner skin. Nevertheless, my father cracked the shells, pierced the skin, and cooked the eggs. He served me one, sunny side up. The yolk was darker than that of a hen's egg, and the white was larger than a hen's egg white. "Eat," he said.

I complied gingerly, picking at the egg with the tip of a fork. I ate the whole thing, reluctantly.

Whenever I went outside, I didn't look into the straw of the coop. I didn't want to find an egg and have to turn it over to my father.

Presently, the duck began to fade. She spent her time sitting in the straw that lined her coop. Maybe she was brooding over her eggs; more likely, she was depressed from her captivity.

My father transferred her to the house cellar, where she did even worse. The darkness and dampness got to her. Now and then, my father went down to feed her, but otherwise she received no attention.

I wanted to free the duck from the basement. I found a large cardboard box and gathered my brother and sister to help me. We descended to the damp, stone-walled room and pulled a string attached to a bare light bulb. The duck was sitting on the dirt floor. She didn't get up when she saw us.

My brother and I carried the duck to the nearby creek; our sister followed. I had the idea that the bird would find a new life in the stream. She was a descendant of wild mallard ducks, bred by the Chinese to be white and relatively tame.

She still didn't stand up when we placed her on the ground, so we put her in the water. She floated slowly away, with her neck extended and her head up. When she reached a distance from us, she looked like a white flower bobbing on the surface.

Killing Jar

M<small>Y FATHER TOLD ME ABOUT A DREAM HE'D HAD.</small> "I was chasing a butterfly," he said. "It was flying just out of reach, and I was running behind. I had no net, only my bare hands. I jumped and grabbed at it."

My father was lying on his bed. I was standing in the doorway, and the room was dark, though it was midafternoon. The sunlight was hidden by window shades. I couldn't tell if my father was looking at me. My brother and sister were outside, and my mother was at work.

"I'm the only one around here who appreciates beautiful things," my father said.

I pictured my father running across a field, with his arms out, as a large butterfly bounced in front of him. I had never seen him run.

———

I went downstairs to my father's workroom. The small space had a linoleum floor and papered walls. I didn't know what the room had been used for before we'd moved in—maybe storage. Several "mounting boards" lay on a metal tabletop. Each board was scored with a lengthwise groove, and dried butterflies rested in the grooves, their wings spread with black pins. Most of the butterflies were right side up, so the tops of their wings were visible. Others, however, were mounted the opposite way—because the undersides of their wings were brightly colored.

Also on the tabletop was a plain-glass vessel with a screw top and a layer of hardened plaster on the bottom. A couple of butterflies were lying motionless on the plaster, their wings folded. I took them out and set them on a mounting board, but I didn't stretch or pin them. I left them for my father to find.

Presently, my father came into the workroom. He didn't explain why he'd been sleeping in midday. When he saw me with the glass container, he said, "That's a killing jar."

He took the jar and picked up a pharmacy bottle. He dripped clear liquid onto the plaster. "All you need," he said, "is a little carbon tetrachloride.

"Some people use carbon tet to clean hats," he added.

When he left the room, I tested the jar. I opened the lid and put the glass flush to my face. I inhaled and became dizzy. The smell was sharp and powerful, but it was not unpleasant— not unpleasant at all. I took my face out of the jar, replaced the lid, and screwed it on tight.

⁓

With the killing jar in a sack and a butterfly net in my hand, I walked outside, crossed the town's one street, and followed a dirt lane between fields. Many butterflies started up, but I didn't chase them. I didn't want to run through prickly weeds.

I wondered if I could use the jar to extinguish other creatures. Anything that could fit in the jar was fair game. Small rodents would do, but I saw none—I didn't have an eagle's eye. Ants were too small, bees could sting, and no exotic bugs or beetles appeared. I didn't see why I was carrying a net and a jar filled with carbon-tet fumes.

—

At night, I woke to the sound of flapping wings. I followed the sound as it went from one wall to the other, just beneath the ceiling. I didn't know what had come in—an insect, a bird, a bat? I turned on the lamp next to my child-size desk. I left the light on and went back to bed, and presently the flapping stopped. At the same time, something eclipsed the light from the lamp. I saw a set of wings spread across the lampshade. At the center of the wings was a small round body, with a large pair of feathery antennae. The creature stayed glued to the shade.

In the morning, I wanted to tell my father about the sighting. I wanted to say, "It was a giant, a goliath. It was the witch moth!"

But my father wasn't the kind of person I could easily approach. He talked to me when he was ready. He summoned me when he had something to say, some lesson to give, usually when he was coming off a drinking binge. Then I could go to his doorway and try to engage him.

Lampblack

I SAW THAT MY FATHER HAD BOUGHT A KEROSENE LAMP—
I guessed he would use it when our electricity went out.
I knew that he liked old-fashioned things and might find its
antique shape and dim glow comforting. Moreover, he had no
income—my mother worked at a hospital job—so he would
appreciate the savings in electricity. He burned the lamp in
the kitchen at night while he drank. I imagined the lamp was
still glowing when he fell asleep at the table.

As soon as I saw the lamp, I wanted to experiment with it. I
brought the appliance to my bedroom, turned up the flat wick
with the key on the metal base, and lit the soaked cotton with
a match. The flame licked the inside of the glass chimney and
gave off a black smoke. I turned the wick up as far as it would
go and held my open hand over the glass. My palm was soon
coated with carbon.

Aside from watching the lamp, there wasn't much for me
to do at night. I usually stayed up late, after my brother and
sister had gone to sleep. Then I would leave our house and
walk along the empty street. At the first streetlight, I could
turn right onto a dirt lane. Where the lane passed through an
unfarmed field, the view would open up, and, if the sky was

clear, I would be able to see stars. The Milky Way would stretch like a band of haze directly overhead. But I didn't really want to go out. Wherever I walked, I would not see anyone. I would have no company. I was fairly comfortable in my room, watching lampblack collect on the glass near the glowing wick.

My father retrieved the lamp. When I walked by his studio, I saw the object on his worktable and a still-life painting on an easel nearby. The lamp was floating in the center of the canvas, over two intersecting lines. The lines were drawn at right angles, one vertical, the other horizontal. All of the edges were sharp.

When my father saw me looking at the painting, he said, "This is what I was meant to do, but this is what I cannot do, because I have a family. I spend my time working for you, not working for myself. I'll give you some advice: Don't ever have a family."

I took the lamp to school for a presentation in speech class. The assignment was to persuade my audience—my classmates—to do something. I stood at the front of the room with the lamp in my hands. "You might not have one of these yet," I said, "but someday you might need one. What are you going to do when the lights go out? Do you have a flashlight? What happens when the batteries die? You'll need a light, and not just a match or a candle. You'll need the biggest burner you can find—a kerosene lamp!"

I held out the lamp and twisted the key. "You can adjust the wick," I continued "You can go from a low flame to the highest flame you've ever seen! The kerosene will last for days, and it's cheaper than gasoline. When you're trapped by a storm, you can sit and stare at the flame. You'll see things you've never seen. You'll see the beginning, and you'll see the end."

I pulled out a box of matches and started to strike one, but the teacher stopped me. "There's no fire allowed in the school," he said.

After my speech, the teacher asked the class to vote. Everyone who was persuaded to acquire a kerosene lamp was invited to raise his or her hand. No one responded.

"It's hard to get no votes at all," the teacher said to me. "Your speech had a strong effect."

In the hallway after class, a girl asked me, "Can you use the lamp to attract moths?"

"I think so," I said.

"Let's take it out one night." she said.

—

As a test, I set the burning lamp on my windowsill after dark. I could imagine a moth being drawn to the light: The moth would see a flame, or multiple flames, through its compound eyes. The image would be a kaleidoscope of light fragments radiating from the wick's tip. The moth would have been navigating by the moon, but the moon would be hidden, and the lamp would be the next-best thing. The moth would have no choice but to fly toward the light; that's what moths were hardwired to do. But the moth would encounter an obstacle: a pane of glass between its body and the flame. Perhaps this development would be lucky; the moth would not fly into the flame and be burned alive. It would settle on the outside of my window and rest its wings.

I tried to call the girl from school, but her mother answered the phone. "Why are you calling?" she asked.

"Your daughter is in my class. We want to take my lamp out at night."

"Why?"

"To attract moths."

"How would that work?"

"The flame will act like the moon."

"You're making no sense," the mother said and hung up.

⁓

During the next storm, our electricity went out—it happened at night. My father walked through the house with a flashlight, fetching candles and setting them in saucers. He gave one candle each to my brother, sister, and mother. But he could not find the kerosene lamp. I saw the blinking of the flashlight, so I picked up the lamp, rolled out the wick, and lit it. The flame was of medium size, but it was brighter than any candle. I brought the lamp to the living room, put it down, and waited for the rest of my family to gather around.

Days of Rain

RAIN HAD BEEN FALLING—THE CLOUDS WERE SO THICK I couldn't see the mountain on the other side of the valley. At one point, the rain stopped and hail fell. I went out to the mown grass and saw ice pellets the size of marbles. Thunder came, and one of our pet dogs hid from the sound. He crawled under a chair and looked upward.

I could imagine what the dog was thinking. He feared the same thing I feared: Each lightning bolt was aimed directly at us. At some point, one of those shots would hit, and we would die. But I couldn't hide under furniture. That sort of escape would have looked suspicious, as if I were losing my grip. So I sat in my room and waited out the storm. In the bedroom, it was just me and my mouse. The mouse ran happily on its exercise wheel, oblivious to the blasts outside. To pass the time, I drew a diagram of a maze that I would build to test the mouse's memory. The mouse would enter from the outside, make turns, retreat from dead ends, and proceed to the middle, where it would find its reward—a chunk of cheese. But I stopped what I was doing when I heard my father calling my name.

I walked slowly to my father's "library" and waited for him to speak. He was hunched over his drawing table, almost asleep. I saw that he had set up a portable screen—a paneled divider that balanced on the floor.

"It's time for your confession," he said. "You can either sit behind the screen, or you can face me. Take your pick."

I sat behind the screen.

"What sins have you committed?" he asked.

"I don't know," I said.

"You'll address me as Father."

"I don't know, Father," I said.

"I saw you go into your bedroom and shut the door. Why did you shut it?" he asked.

"I was doing an experiment."

"Doing an experiment, *what*?"

"Doing an experiment, Father."

"Right, you were 'doing an experiment.' That's a sin!"

I looked around the part of the room that wasn't blocked by the screen. Books filled the floor-to-ceiling shelves, and an easel held a half-painted canvas.

"I'm going to tell you how to make up for your sin," my father said.

He came around to my side of the screen. "You see these books on the shelves? You'll clean each one of them."

He gave me a paintbrush with soft bristles. "You'll take each book and dust it with this brush, then you'll put it back in its place. When you're finished, you'll pray for forgiveness."

I pulled out a book and saw that the top was covered with dust. I whisked at the edges of the pages with the paintbrush, then took a cloth and rubbed the cover. I repeated the task a few times, but I couldn't get through even one shelf of books. My father had gone, so I left without saying the prayer.

～

I went back to my bedroom and took care not to shut the door. In the room, it was still me and my mouse. I put water in the bottle in the rodent's cage, and he lapped at the tip of the spout. I could see his tongue moving quickly. Then he climbed onto his wheel and ran. The wheel squeaked; it needed oil. But I fell asleep despite the noise. When I woke in the middle of the night, the mouse was still running on the wheel.

～

In the morning, I saw my mother practicing Tai Chi. "It helps my arthritis," she said.

"How did you learn?" I asked.

"I learned by watching old people when I was a child. They exercised in parks all over the city."

She held her hands palm-out in front of her and twisted at the waist. She stepped back as she formed a circle with her arms. She pointed to the ceiling with one hand and down to the floor with the other, then brought her arms to her sides. She called out the names of the positions: "Repulse Monkey … Carry Tiger to Mountain … Diagonal Flying."

I picked up my mouse-maze diagram and walked out to catch the school bus.

～

In science class, I explained my experiment. I would build a maze from cardboard and make paper copies of the map I'd drawn. I would send the mouse into the pathways and trace its route on paper with a red pencil. I would count how many times the mouse attempted to find the cheese before he succeeded, or before he gave up.

"Did you come up with this idea on your own," the teacher asked, "or did you have help?"

"On my own," I said.

"Your drawing is too sophisticated," the teacher said. "Your father must have helped you. You fail this project."

⏤

As I walked past a girl in the hallway, she said, "You look like Bruce Lee."

I struck a Tai Chi pose, one that I'd seen my mother take. I moved my hands outward from an imaginary centerline. "This is called Part Horse's Mane," I said.

"I'm not dating Bruce Lee," the girl said.

As I walked away, I heard students chanting, "Bruce! Bruce! Bruce!"

⏤

Rain fell for a few days straight, and a creek formed on the hill behind our house. The creek was supposed to run through a culvert under the roadway, but the culvert was blocked. I looked out a window and thought the grass in our yard had turned brown. But I wasn't seeing grass; I was seeing floodwater.

I knew about the trough that would funnel the water away from our yard. If it could be opened, the water would drain away. I needed help, so I went to find my father. He was in his studio, bent over his drawing table. On the tabletop sat a can of tobacco and a bottle of beer. When he saw me, he said, "When the sun disappears, I want to die."

I told him about the flooded yard and the jammed culvert, and he accompanied me outside. We saw that the outflow pipe was clogged with tree branches. Tearing them out took a lot of strength and energy. We made progress, however, and the yard started to empty like a bathtub. The water was gone in about a half hour.

Hunting for Bait

A S SOON AS IT WAS DARK OUTSIDE, MY FATHER SHOWED me how to hunt for fishing worms. He gave me a flashlight, took another for himself, and led me to the wet grass behind my family's house. Here and there, we spotted the tip of a night crawler, glistening with moisture. "Walk softly," my father whispered, "and keep your light pointed away."

I stepped cautiously, looking for earthworms that I could grab before they retreated. For a while, all I saw were shiny "heads" that quickly disappeared. Then I saw a healthy specimen halfway exposed. I crept up and jabbed down with my fingers. "Don't pull too hard," my father advised, "or you'll break it."

I eased the worm out of the soil, then placed it, squirming, into a jar.

In another spot, I saw two night crawlers pressed together. The creatures were pointed in opposite directions, with their tails still in the ground. I moved fast and pinched both worms in a fist before they could slide away.

"They were mating," father explained. "Worms are all the same, but it takes two to reproduce. You got two for one."

My father went back into the house, and I continued searching. The earthworms I found were each about nine inches long. I didn't see any that were giants, like the three-foot species in Australia. I'd seen photos of men with such worms draped over their outstretched hands. What kind of fish would take a three-foot earthworm, anyway? A whale shark? A barracuda? I would have been happy to catch a trout of legal size—six inches or longer.

I put several night crawlers and a handful of wet grass into a plastic bait box. The lid was perforated to let in air, so the worms could breathe through their skin.

When I came back into the house, I saw my father sitting in the kitchen. An empty shot glass, a bottle of whiskey, and a half-empty bottle of beer were on the table. "You'd better go fishing while you can," he said, "because the oilmen are planning to dig up the stream. They need that area for fracking. You'll see a conversion plant instead of a trout run."

"I'm going out in the morning," I said.

"You know what happens when the fracking waste gets into the drinking supply?" my father asked. "You turn on the faucet, and water mixed with sand comes out!"

Upstairs, my mother was ironing. She had a board set up against the wall opposite a beige chifforobe. The light from the hallway came into my bedroom, but I didn't shut the door because I didn't want my father to see it closed and accuse me of something.

"I'm on call tonight," my mother said. She meant the phone could ring and she would have to go to the hospital to do lab work. If there was an accident, she would have to cross-match blood for a transfusion. She was ironing so she would have a pressed uniform.

Later in the night, I heard the phone ring for my mother, but I didn't get out of bed before she left.

When I went downstairs in the morning, I saw that my father was still at the kitchen table. He had bent forward on his chair so he could rest his head. He had added a few more bottles to his collection, and he was snoring. My mother hadn't returned from the hospital.

My sister wasn't up yet, but my brother was awake. I asked him to go with me to the nearby creek, and he agreed. We walked to a place where the stream passed under a wooden bridge, then cut under tree roots. I tried to picture a fracking plant where the bridge lay—a pressurized tank and a wastewater pool, connected by a network of pipes—then switched to the task at hand. I put a worm on a hook and worked the bait through the riffles next to the bank. Almost immediately, a fish struck hard—nothing other than a trout would hit that way. I was eager and tried to set the hook; I could feel the weight and strength of the fish. I pulled up, and the fish came toward the surface. It rose in silver-blue flashes. Then it dropped from my line and vanished into the dark water. It would not strike again. It would lurk next to the stream bank until the fracking plant arrived.

At home, my sister was sitting at the kitchen table, and my father was frying food at the stove. I could smell bacon. The beer bottles were still on the table. I glanced at one of my father's paintings on the wall. In the picture, a girl was skipping rope. She had straight black hair, and she was wearing shorts and a T-shirt. The rope was set at the top of its arc over her head, and her elbows formed perfect V's. One foot was raised in the middle of a skip. She looked like a stylized version of my sister.

I took my bait box to the backyard, opened the lid, and poked at the wet grass inside. I found the remaining night crawlers in a clump at the bottom, keeping their skins wet so they could breathe. When I touched them, they reacted with twitches. I dumped them out on the lawn, where they might crawl back into the earth. If the night was cold and damp, they would come back out of the ground, perhaps to find a counterpart and mate.

Artificial Lure

MY FATHER CALLED ME TO THE KITCHEN. I CAME INTO the large, wallpapered room and stood behind him while he dissected a fish on a cutting board. I had caught the trout earlier in the day; its guts were now spread out on the surface. A small fluorescent light illuminated the counter. My father poked at the internal organs with the point of a knife. He found the stomach and sliced it open. "Look," he said, as he removed a ball of tiny pebbles. "It's a caddis fly larva, wrapped in gravel. The fish ate the larva and its casing."

He removed some unidentifiable adult insects, maybe crickets or grasshoppers, but they were now twisted and black. "Later," he said, "I'll show you how to tie a dry fly to mimic an adult caddis fly, with wings."

As promised, my father gave me a fly-tying lesson in his work space. He loosened the jaws of a vise, then clamped a fishhook between the metal pieces. He tied a couple of feathers to the hook with thread, then wound the feathers around the shaft so that the bristles stuck out. He dropped glue onto the ends of the tiny bouquet. "Here, you have a dun," he said. "Trout feed on duns— sometimes they go into a frenzy. The duns live only for a day."

My father set up an unadorned hook. "Your turn," he said.

I tried to duplicate what he'd made, but I couldn't attach the feather to the hook, wrap it tightly, or glue the thread neatly.

"You need to try something easier," my father said, "like a bucktail streamer."

He gave me a bigger hook and showed me how to attach the hairs from a deer's tail to the front of the wire, then wrap thread around the hairs and glue the ends. The finished streamer looked like a puffy minnow.

After my father had left the room, I experimented with the vise. I put a fishing bobber between the jaws and turned the screw. The plastic ball distended into an ovoid shape, then exploded. The sound was louder than the pop of a pierced balloon. I looked for other objects I could crush in the vise: a handheld eraser, a lemon, a light bulb.

⁓

At the dinner table, my father went on a rant. "I'm always fixing things," he said as he shook his fork. "Now, my fly-tying vise doesn't work. It's jammed."

My mother, wearing an apron, stood on the other side of the kitchen. "When I was a child," she said, "I never saw people fishing with flies. There were fishermen on boats on the lake. They used nets to catch *niányú*, a fish with whiskers."

"A catfish has whiskers," I said, "and poison spines."

"The lake was made by a dragon," she said. "Only a dragon could dig a trench that deep."

"We didn't do it," my siblings said.

"I don't care who did it!" my father shouted. "First I amuse. Then I fix. Do I have time for stretching canvases? For making paintings? For showing my artwork in galleries? No, I don't.

All I have time for is entertaining children. Do they appreciate it? Do they learn anything? No."

He stood up then and walked out the door. I hoped he would stay late at the bar and not wake us when he returned.

In the morning, I took my fly rod and my streamer and walked to the nearby stream. I found a stretch of water that split off from the main channel. The runaround looked deep enough to hide a fish—the water was green. I climbed down rocks and crouched on the bank. Behind me was a cow pasture and, beyond that, a dirt road. I threw the streamer into the water and worked it with the rod tip so that it swam like a minnow. If I caught a trout, I thought, I might check its stomach to see what it had been eating.

I didn't want to be seen. I didn't want to hear someone coming toward me. After a while, however, a boy on a tractor spotted me. He seemed to be on an errand, between one field and another. He stopped the tractor and let it idle. "Ah so!" he called over the chugging engine.

I didn't know if I should stay where I was or walk away.

"It's a hot day. Where's your coolie hat?"

He turned the tractor's steering wheel in my direction. I expected him to charge toward me. I felt in my fishing sack for a weapon, but all I had was a fish scaler. The tool wasn't sharp. It would just scrape the skin—and remove any scales that were there.

After a few moments, the boy put the tractor in gear and rolled away.

I started to walk home, along the one street of the town. Outside an old wooden house, an elderly man saw me. "Did you catch anything?" he asked.

I patted the canvas sack that hung from my shoulder.

"You always catch something," he said.

Angry God

I COULD HEAR MY PARENTS ARGUING. WE HAD FINISHED supper, and I was sitting between them and the TV set. My brother and sister were watching a show, and I was doing my homework on the couch arm. The show was about a train stop off the main line, where three young women used a water tower as a bathtub. During the opening credits, their undergarments were hanging over the edge of the giant tank. The theme song promised "curves" on the rail track, and even more curves at the train's destination.

Now and then, my parents' voices came over the sound of the television.

"God is angry with me," my father said. "I must have done something wrong. It must have been having a family. I can't take care of a family. I'm supposed to make my art."

"Don't talk to me about religion," my mother said. "I'm the daughter of a Chinese minister."

"An angry God makes me angry. Why can't I have a long stride, like the stride of the God who stomps out nations?"

"'The foolishness of God is greater than man's wisdom.'"

"Don't quote the Bible to me. I'm keeping it away from my children. The Devil is talking to me now."

"I'm going to mark the page about wisdom with a gold tassel."

On the TV, the mother was warning her three daughters about danger around the bend. A train crew might sneak in and drain the water tower, leaving the women "bare."

"I'm not taking my kids to church," my father said. "They're not going to be Americans."

"Are they going to be Chinese?" my mother asked. "Will they eat from an iron rice bowl?"

"They will eat what we can grow and catch."

—

I headed out of the house, toward an abandoned sawmill that lay at the end of a dirt road. I walked along an embankment where a railroad track used to run. The path was overgrown with weeds, but other hikers had worn a track through the stalks. I passed a wooden shed, where logs had been cut and stacked next to a railroad siding. Some of the logs were still there, but the building had no water tower, and no women bathing. Such thoughts, I realized, might bring the wrath of God, but I pictured the bare women anyway.

I had a fishing rod in one hand and a creel slung over a shoulder. I walked to the bank of the stream to avoid the underbrush and came to a place where a tree trunk curved over the water—the bole was easy to stand on. From there, I threw my lure into the water, and the "minnow" floated quickly downstream. I pulled it back, feeling it wiggling against the current.

Mosquitoes flew around me. They were so small I could barely see them, but if one touched my skin, it would bite and inject its saliva. I would feel a slight stab and scratch the spot, and a white lump would appear.

Presently, my brother showed up. I looked at his face to see what was happening at home. "Is he still angry?" I asked.

"Yes."

We walked out of the undergrowth and into a meadow, looking into the water for fish. The problem was, the fish saw us before we saw them. When we came to slow-moving stretches, we frightened whole schools. They raced away together, in a pattern for protection. While I had space to cast a lure, there was nothing to aim for—the trout were gone.

On our way home, my brother and I passed the only church in town: a small brick building with a large parking lot for the congregation. "Have you ever been inside?" my brother asked.

"No," I said.

"I was in there once, for a Boy Scout meeting. They thought I was going to join, but I didn't go back."

⁓

At home, I saw that my father was out at the local bar.

"My Bible is missing," my mother said. "I think someone stole it."

"Who would do that?" I asked.

"A couple of Jehovah's Witnesses came to the door, and I let them in. You know them. One of them is in your class at school."

"I don't think they took it," I said.

"My edition has drawings in the margins. It's an illustrated manuscript."

⁓

On my ride to school, the bus stopped for the boy who was a Jehovah's Witness. When he got on, I asked him if he'd seen a fancy Bible, an illustrated edition. "My mother is missing hers," I said.

"We have our own Bibles," he said, "with our own scripture. We don't observe pagan holidays, like you do."

At the beginning of the school day, I stood for the Pledge of Allegiance and recited the words with my hand over my heart. But the Jehovah's Witness stood silently, with his arms at his sides.

—

In the evening I felt hot, and my skin was itchy from mosquito bites. I started to watch the TV show about the young women who lived at the end of the train line. In this episode, one of them climbed into the locomotive cab and took the throttle, then proceeded to drive the train.

I went into the bathroom and lay on the linoleum floor. The hard surface was cool and soothing. I reclined on my back, then switched to my front. Lying on the front of my body was more comfortable; I pressed my skin against the floor.

I wasn't like other people. They wouldn't lie on the floor. They probably had nicer floors anyway, made of materials other than linoleum. I rubbed against the hard surface. Soon, an urge overwhelmed me; I had to start scratching.

Casting Votes

MY HIGH-SCHOOL SPANISH TEACHER TOLD THE CLASS he was looking forward to the upcoming U.S. presidential election. He said that "*los Demócratas*" had been in office for eight years. It was time for a change to "*los Republicanos.*" He wanted to know what the students thought. I hoped he wouldn't notice me, but he pointed to me for an answer.

I stood and said, "I don't think so. I mean, *Creo que no.*"

"*Gracias, Tomás,*" the teacher said, using my Spanish name. "You can take your seat now. It's time for a change, time for *un cambio.*"

After class, I told a girl who sat next to me that I wanted to switch my Spanish name to Santiago. "I don't like Tomás," I said. "I like Santiago better."

"What does it mean?" she asked.

"It means 'Saint Iago.' He may have been Jesus' cousin."

"There's no way I'm calling you that," she said.

⁓

At home, my father ranted to my family about the upcoming election. "Capitalism has had its day," he said as we sat at the supper table. "Soon, we'll vote out the fat cats, and we'll have socialism. After that comes communism. We'll have no private property. My neighbor can come to my house and take what he needs. If he wants my fishing pole, he can take it. If he needs my car, he can take that, too, as long as he gives it back.

"I'll need to stock up soon," my father added, "so I can be ready for shortages when the revolution comes. I'm going to the beer distributor today."

He had one beer that I could see. It was a long-necked, brown-glass bottle, standing next to his plate.

"I'm a Chinese immigrant," my mother said. "I can't vote."

"The East is Red," my father said. "Mao came to save the Chinese people."

"He installed indoor plumbing," my mother said. "I never liked going to the bathroom outside."

"Where did you go?" my sister asked.

"We had a latrine. It supplied nutrients for the fields."

"Mao was a leader," my father said, "the first real leader since the Great Khan. He was no peacemaker. He built toilets, lots of them."

"He got rid of open sewage," my mother said. "I was always afraid of getting dysentery."

"A revolution is not a garden party," my father said.

⌣

Realizing how lucky we were, I took notice of our bathroom. The space had not been a bathroom originally. It had been a large closet or a small bedroom. The previous resident had broken through the floor and ceiling and had installed pipes and drains for a toilet, sink, and bathtub. A potbellied stove sat on the floor; a radiator stood under a window. The stove wasn't in use anymore; a coal furnace pumped hot water through the radiator during cold months. Through the window I could see a dead tree—only the trunk and one large branch were left. It had been a chokecherry, and was still standing.

⁓

My father planted a sign in the ground at the front of our house. The placard carried the name of the Democratic candidate for president. The next day, I saw that someone had written "COMMIE" on the cardboard. The day after that, I noticed the sign was gone. All that was left was a hole in the ground.

⁓

When I returned to Spanish class, I listened to the teacher talk about his favored candidate. "Who do you want in the White House? Some peacenik who's going to turn tail? Or someone who's going to go in there and win the war?"

I told the teacher I wanted to be called Santiago.

"What's wrong with Tomás?"

"Well, my name isn't Thomas. How about San Tomás?"

"San Tomás," the teacher said. "It sounds like a place. We have a student named Frank. We'll call him San Francisco."

⁓

Later, I saw the girl from Spanish class in the hallway. "I'm not Santiago anymore," I said to her, "Now I'm San Tomás."

"I'm not calling you that, either," she said.

⁓

After school, I walked to the local fire hall—the closest polling place. The ladder trucks had been rolled out of the garage, and long tables had been set up inside. I was too young to vote, so I waited next to the trucks and watched people going in and out. I didn't know who they were voting for, but I was sure they supported *los Republicanos*. They didn't care who the candidate was, as long as he was from that party. At one point, I saw my father come out of the building.

"Who did you vote for?" I asked

"There was no one I liked," he said, "but there was a Communist on the ballot."

"Did you vote for the Communist?"

"No, I voted for the Democrat, even though he doesn't have a chance."

My father and I walked back up the narrow street—past wooden houses, the post office, and the hotel bar—toward our house. We didn't see any of our neighbors on the way, but I had a feeling they were watching us through their windows.

—

In our yard, the dead chokecherry tree had been knocked down. I couldn't picture how it had happened. There might have been a strong wind, maybe a tornado, but I remembered no storm. Vandals might have toppled it with strong kicks. Or the rotting wood might have just given out.

"We'll save the tree trunk and the branches," my father said. "We'll chop them up for firewood. We might need to use that potbellied stove in the bathroom when the Republicans take over."

Bun Dong

M Y MOTHER TOLD ME THE CHINESE NEW YEAR WAS ABOUT to begin. The first new moon on the lunar calendar was approaching. And a beneficent animal was coming; it would help those under its sign for the next twelve months.

I wondered if, at the moment of transition, we would see fireworks, gather in a crowd, and shout into the night sky.

"In the city where I grew up," she said, "children would go out to a street—there was one special street—and get a glass toy. It looked like a wide bottle, and when you blew into it, the bottom would snap in and out."

I could picture the glass bottom changing from concave to convex with the air from a breath.

"The name of the toy was the sound it made, *bun dong*. We would hear this all day: *bun dong, bun dong*. But the glass would easily break, and you were lucky to have a whole toy by the end of the day."

At night, I opened our front door and looked across the narrow street. The darkness wasn't total over a mown cornfield—patches of ice glowed with reflected light. Maybe the source was the Milky Way, but more likely it was a streetlight attached to a telephone pole. To either side of our front steps was a house with lit windows. One neighbor had a Confederate flag hanging over his porch.

I scanned the sky for the moon but couldn't find it. Maybe it had risen in total shadow, or maybe it hadn't risen at all.

I took a wide-bottom flask from my chemistry set and tried to fashion a *bun dong* toy. The glass was rigid, unresponsive to my deep breaths. However, I could blow across the top of the flask to make notes. I could pour water into the container to change the pitch and produce a melody. With my talent, I could join a jug band. But I wanted a New Year's noisemaker. An empty water bottle wouldn't work—the plastic didn't have enough snap. I needed something tinnier. An empty tuna can fit well over my face, but when I inhaled and exhaled, the bottom surface did not pop.

I went into my parents' bedroom and rooted in my mother's trunk, looking for a sample of the glass toy. The box was filled with clothing—silk dresses in bright colors, high-heeled shoes, hand fans. I contemplated the clothing, rubbing the fabric between my fingers. The bright-blue and -red colors matched those of the Confederate flag on our neighbor's house.

I stopped when my mother came in. She took an ink drawing from the trunk and smoothed it with her hand. "The rice paper got wrinkled during my boat trip to America," she explained.

In the middle of the drawing was a bamboo stalk with black pointed leaves. On the bottom right were four characters. "The writing means 'Drawing shapes, drawing colors,' or 'Drawing music, drawing colors,'" my mother said.

I wanted to make musical notes and that rose like colors. I went into my father's workroom and found a tiny drum: a miniature bongo with a handle. It had balls on strings that would hit the skins when the handle was rolled between one's palms. The repeated sound was satisfying—I could send the thumps a long way. I went out to the street and began to drum up a storm.

Presently, the neighbor with the Confederate flag opened his door and stepped onto his porch. He was wearing a sheriff's uniform. "What the hell are you doing?" he shouted.

"Celebrating," I said. "My year is coming."

"Well, knock it off."

I quit the drumming.

Marionette

WHEN MY FATHER CALLED MY NAME, I WENT TO HIS unheated workroom at the back of the house. There, he had a sheet of wood clamped in a vice, and he'd spilled a lot of sawdust on the floor. He handed me a coping saw. "Use it," he said, "to make curves."

I drew the thin blade back and forth across the wood piece. My cut wasn't a curve, but it wasn't straight, either; it was a zigzag.

"Stand and watch," my father said. "This is how you execute a project."

I looked around the room. Dozens of canvases were propped against the walls. An easel stood in the middle of the floor. On my father's worktable was an assortment of wood pieces: a disk, sticks of different lengths, a rectangular block. Each piece had screw eyes sunk into it.

—

The next day, my father presented a marionette to my two siblings and me. We got up from where we were watching TV to look at the toy. "Now," he said, "you don't need to watch the idiot box. You can write a story. You can put on a show."

The marionette was about two feet high and resembled a clown. My father had covered the figure in a harlequin costume. For the face, he'd inked cartoony features onto the wooden disk—the expression was one of surprise. The marionette had no hair, but wore a floppy hat with points. Its torso was the rectangular block of wood. My father handed me two crisscrossed sticks with strings leading to the head, elbows, and knees. When I tilted the handles, the marionette lifted his hands and feet.

But the marionette didn't behave well. He flapped his arms, jumped up, and fell down. His strings became tangled, and soon he couldn't move at all. I rolled him backwards in a somersault to untangle the strings, but that only made the snarl worse. He hung from the handles, with one knee and one elbow permanently raised. I hooked him to a nail on the wall and left him there.

⁓

I went to an empty room upstairs. Like my father's workroom, this room had no heat. I opened a door that led onto the porch roof. I didn't know why a door would lead from the room to a roof, but this door did. The temperature outside was slightly colder than inside. I stood on the roof, stepped toward the edge, and looked down. The grass in the yard was brittle and yellow, and was covered with dried leaves and the brown husks of tree nuts. I walked on the roof to the front of the house. Tacked to the outside wall was a cord of Christmas lights I'd put up a couple of years earlier. I'd wanted to spell the word PEACE with the lights, but I didn't have enough lights, so I spelled PAX. At least, the word wasn't POX. I hadn't plugged in the lights after that first season. As I walked around, I tried to look in through the windows, but the shades were drawn. I didn't think anyone was inside, anyway. My brother, sister and father were up and out of bed, and my mother had left early for work. I could see the one street of the town and the neighboring houses: a wooden duplex with faded white paint, a tarpapered structure with a plastic sheet for a front door, a newly built brick split-level. In the distance was the forested hill we called Rattlesnake Mountain. I'd never seen a venomous snake anywhere in the area, though I supposed a rattlers' nest could lie among the glacial boulders at the top of the hill.

I stood on the roof until I felt very cold.

At supper, my father said, "I remember when bread cost a dime. During the war, we recycled rubber, metal, and paper. We got paid a few cents per pound. With those few cents, we could buy a loaf of bread.

"You kids don't know what it was like," he continued. "If you want something, we buy it. But who pays for it?"

"Well, I do," my mother said. "I have a job."

"And what do you do there, in the hospital lab? You flirt with a man named Mr. Asspansky."

"Mr. Supansky," my mother said.

"Asspansky!" my father shouted as he hit the table with his fist.

"May I be excused?" I asked.

"You're all dismissed!" my father said.

When I next looked into the kitchen, I saw that my father had left—most likely for the local bar. I didn't know whether to feel abandoned, or relieved that he was gone.

Fortunately, I was asleep when he got back. He might have continued his argument with my mother, picking up where he'd left off about the Casanova in the hospital, but I didn't wake to hear it.

The next day, I started to build a puppet theater out of weathered planks of wood. I wore a coat while I worked with a saw and hammer in the empty upstairs room. The theater was flimsy—it wobbled at a touch—but it stood without collapsing. I would hang a curtain from the top bar, and I would hide behind the frame. But the frame had no backing, so my body would be visible.

I took the marionette from the hook on the wall and gradually untangled the strings. I untied each line from its screw eye, pulled it free, and retied it. After a while, the clown hung loose again. I called my brother and sister to the porch downstairs. "Wait here," I said.

They looked out over the yard while I went upstairs, fetched the marionette, and stepped onto the roof. I held the sticks in front of me and lowered the puppet carefully until it was in my brother's and sister's line of sight. I lifted the tip of one handle, and the marionette's right arm went up. I lifted the other handle, and his left arm rose. I proceeded to make one knee, then the other, move. "He's running from demons," I explained.

"Where are the demons?" my brother asked.

"I don't see any demons," my sister said.

The marionette jogged, but he didn't get very far. He highstepped in the air next to the porch. He twisted and turned, and the points on his jester hat bounced. His cartoon face remained frozen in an expression of surprise.

"The demons are in your head," I said.

Into the Box

I FOUND SOME SCRAPS OF WOOD IN MY FATHER'S STUDIO AND decided to make a box. I picked up a flat piece that was the right shape for the base. To fashion a container, I could glue slats around the sides and attach either a sliding or a hinged piece for the top. I started by cutting the sides to length with a coping saw.

When my brother saw me working, he asked, "What are you making?"

"A box," I said.

"What for?"

"To keep my collections."

In a drawer, I had a few pieces of shale with seashell fossils embedded in them. The shells were common types—clams or snails—from the time when a sea covered the land where we lived. I could store the fossils in the box.

⁓

When I heard my father yelling at my mother, I worked on the box. I sanded the wood pieces, then applied lacquer. I didn't put the pieces together; I left them on a tabletop to dry.

My father was repeating a line he'd heard in a movie: "What we have here is a failure to communicate." His voice became louder with each iteration.

Using a pencil, I sketched a diagram showing how the pieces would fit together.

"When I speak," my father shouted, "you listen!"

My mother said something in reply, but her voice was too soft for me to make out the words.

I heard my father say, "He's a fairy."

"What do you mean?" my mother asked.

"He's a small creature with wings."

—

I checked my nipples and discovered that they had grown larger. Each nipple had a small lump behind it, which made the dark tip protrude. I wondered if I was sprouting breasts. Such a development would mean I wasn't a man. At best, I would be a hermaphrodite, a she-male. With the Asian features I'd gotten from my mother, I would be a dragon man-lady.

There weren't many Asian hermaphrodites around. If I became one, I wouldn't fit into society as I knew it. I might belong in a sideshow—that would be where I could be myself. I could be part of a circus community.

I put on a T-shirt but made sure it wasn't too tight. If it clung to my skin, the contours of my torso would show. If I were around my family—riding in our car, say—they might look at my chest and see my budding nipples.

—

My mother gave me a shirt made of slippery material. It had a wide collar, and it fit close to the body. It was a disco shirt.

"I want to exchange it," I said.

My mother gave me a ride to a clothing store. On the way, she said, "Your father can't be creative unless he drinks. When he gets drunk, he gets ideas. The drunker he gets, the more bright thoughts he gets."

When we arrived at the store, I went straight to the flannel shirts. I picked a baggy one, and my mother bought it for me.

At home, my father noticed my new shirt. "Now you're a lumberjack," he said. "Why don't you go out and chop some wood?"

I picked up a hatchet and took it outside. There was a living tree in the backyard, but the hatchet didn't do much damage, even when I swung hard. The branches flexed, and the heavy blade just bounced off.

I had to find some dry wood. Old sticks were lying on the ground. A couple of blows against a lengthwise stick would sever it. But the best wood to split was a dry plank. The outside of our house was covered with wood siding. I took the hatchet to a slat. The wood split cleanly down the middle, along the grain. I attacked the walls of the house. When I was finished, part of the siding was scored with dents and cracks.

Later, my brother asked me, "Where's that box you were making?" He chuckled as he spoke, as if he knew I'd forgotten the project.

I went back to work on the box but couldn't figure out how to make the top. With my rudimentary skills, I couldn't attach a hinged or sliding piece. So I left the top off. I had a box with a bottom and sides—a tray. I could use the tray to hold things.

My father took me to a local art gallery. The showroom was in a well-kept house next to a paved road in the country.

"Do you remember me?" my father asked the gallery owner when we walked in.

The owner, a large man with dark hair and a black beard, looked at him and said, "No."

"I've lived here for years," my father said.

"So have I."

"I gave you some artwork on consignment," my father said.

"I don't remember it."

The man slid open flat files and found some works on paper. They were silk-screened prints of butterflies.

"I thought these were commercial," my father said.

"You can take them back."

Before we left, we saw a dish that held polished stones—they were as smooth as glass. The dish was next to a bin filled with rough stones. My father paid for a couple of the rough ones.

"I'll set you up with Carborundum powder," my father said to me, "so you can make your own gems."

—

At home, I mixed the abrasive powder with water and went to work on the rough objects. I rubbed them with a cloth soaked in the mixture. After what seemed a long time, I hadn't made much progress. The stones were still dull.

My arms got tired from sanding, so I moved them to loosen the muscles. When I rotated my shoulders, the blade bones stuck out on my back. I looked into a mirror to see if the protrusions were the beginnings of wings. If I didn't have breasts, I might have appendages that I could flap. I would go to a high place to test my wings. I would jump off, then either fly away or drop straight down.

I put the sanded stones, along with pieces of shale containing fossils, into the box I'd constructed. The box still had no top. Everyone could see what I'd collected. If I couldn't get a job in the circus, I might become a gemologist. There might be a call for such an expert, I thought.

Push-Button Knife

PART OF MY HIGH-SCHOOL EDUCATION INVOLVED TRAFFIC safety. Older students served as crossing guards for school-children—we had no professional guards. The prospect of a new role excited me—I wanted that authority. But I had to wait my turn. There were many students who could serve as crossing guards and few intersections that needed guarding.

When my turn came, I was assigned the farthest, least busy intersection. Still, I was excited by my powerful job. I would be treated with respect, though I didn't look like a person in charge.

I waited on a corner for what seemed a long time before a couple of children—who looked to be about six years old—arrived. Seizing my opportunity, I turned toward them and raised my arms as they approached. "Ho!" I said.

With my arms still outstretched, I faced the street and looked right and left, then right again. The small students stood obediently behind me. The street had no traffic, and I couldn't stop traffic anyway. All I could do was protect crossers from being hit. I dropped my arms, gave a hand signal, and said, "Go!"

The children walked forward unharmed.

No other kids showed up during my shift. But a rusty pickup truck sped by, braked up ahead, and rolled back in reverse. The driver had a mullet haircut, a mustache, and a beard. He asked, "Are you selling cookies?"

"No," I said.

"Why not? You're wearing a Girl Scout banner."

"This is a belt and a badge," I said. My uniform was a white-cloth harness that went around my waist and over a shoulder. The silver medallion was pinned to the sash over my chest.

"I want Thin Mints," he said as he revved his engine, "and malted-milk balls. Do you have milk balls?"

"I don't," I said.

"You look like you do."

The driver gunned his engine. White smoke spewed from the truck's tailpipe as he raced away.

⏤

When I got home, I went upstairs to my bedroom, where a small mirror that swiveled in a wooden stand sat on my dresser. Usually, I avoided the mirror—I didn't like to look at my face. But now I angled the mirror so I could see. My features distinguished me from the people around me, distinguished me even from my parents. I couldn't figure out my face or evaluate it, but it was definitely from somewhere else. It partly reminded me of people in my mother's country, China, where everyone had straight black hair, round cheeks, a flat nose, and narrow eyes. But it was also partly similar to the faces of the white American people around me.

I sat at my desk and prepared to sharpen a pencil with the blade of my penknife. When I pulled out the blade with a thumbnail, the metal part swung open slowly. What I wanted was a switchblade, like ones I'd seen in TV movies, with a button you pushed to snap the blade out. With minimal effort, the touch of a finger, the blade was locked and ready. But I didn't know where to get a switchblade. So I drew a picture of one with the pencil I'd sharpened.

———

In school, I showed a nerdy-looking classmate my sketch and said, "I'm looking for a switch."

"What kind of switch?" he asked.

"One that you can open and close automatically," I said.

"You're looking for a switch that you can open and close automatically. A normal on-off switch, with a handle." He nodded as if he knew exactly what I meant.

After class, I stopped at the newsstand in the town where I went to high school. Some magazines had sensational covers that showed victims of crimes, or targets of crimes that had not yet been committed. The photos were meant to arouse the reader. One cover line read, "If you don't buy this magazine, this woman will die!"

I brought out my drawing of a switchblade and showed it to a counter clerk. "What's that?" he asked. "A hair comb? A hot roller?"

"It's a spring-loaded knife," I said.

"We don't sell illegal weapons here," the clerk said.

———

When I arrived at my crossing-guard station the next day, the sidewalk was empty of children. To pass the time, I tried to identify the makes of cars. At first, I could recognize only those that matched my family's car: a Plymouth Valiant. All others looked the same to me, so I developed a method of identification. I studied the shapes of taillights and looked for the model name on the fenders. Round taillights indicated a Ford, while a vertical light on a fin marked a Cadillac or a Buick. But there were exceptions. Ford Lincolns also had vertical taillights, as did some Chryslers. In fact, there were cars with round taillights that were not Fords.

I began to think about what kind of car I might get when I could drive. I wouldn't need anything larger than a two-seater. I wasn't planning to have any passengers. That is, unless I were to have a family. Parents with even one child would require more than a two-seat car.

The same pickup truck that had stopped earlier approached. The driver pulled up and rolled down his window.

"Do you know if there's a gay bar around here?" he asked.

"I don't drink," I said.

"I heard there was a gay bar here."

"Not that I know of," I said.

"Come on," he said. "You know there's a gay bar near here."

The driver drove off fast, hooting through his window. His "Woohoo!" reached me several times before it faded away.

I imagined a place where I could get a push-button knife. I would walk into a flea market, where anyone could sell anything, and see what I was looking for on a table. Someone might have brought it from a state where it was legal. The knife would have a pearl-colored handle and a double-edged blade. The release button would be sensitive to the slightest touch. If I were to carry the knife in my pocket, I would have to be careful not to let it snap open without warning.

"How much?" I would ask.

The price might be high, but I would find a way to pay it.

Seeing the Light

I RODE A SCHOOL BUS TO A NEARBY FARM TO START MY afternoon job. My task was to cut weeds with the blade of a shovel. I walked around a pasture, and wherever I saw a burdock plant I severed the stem at the ground. The idea was to get rid of the prickly seedpods, which would stick to farm animals' fur.

A boy who lived on the farm worked with me. At one point, we saw a group of goats in a neighboring field. Two of the animals were standing apart, eyeing each other. They moved in a circle; then the larger goat rose onto the back of the smaller one. "He's breeding her," the boy explained.

The boy and I went into the barn when we were finished chopping weeds. The large shed smelled of cow manure. All of the cows were locked by their necks to gates in their stalls. Before the farmer began milking, he washed the cows' udders with a cloth and attached metal cups to their teats. The cups drew milk into hoses that led into an adjoining building. Only the adult farmer could hook up the cows—maybe he was the only person the cows would tolerate.

The boy took me into the next building, which held the bulk tank. The stainless-steel cylinder looked like it could contain hundreds of gallons. The boy opened the lid, and I leaned over and looked in. The unpasteurized liquid, thick and pure white, filled the bottom of the tank. The boy scooped some milk into a plastic jug and gave me the container—my payment for working.

—

I wrote a paper for class on how to tell male goats from female goats: "The billy goat has a longer beard than the nanny, though they both have beards. The kids, of course, have the shortest beards. They don't have much of a *goatee*. The ones with the longer goatees breed with each other often and in the open. They are frisky."

When I got my paper back, I noticed that the teacher had addressed me as "Flip."

"Flip," she wrote, "you might think you're funny, but who is the real goat here?"

—

My mother told me she'd seen someone who knew me. "I was in the grocery store," she said, "and she came up to me."

"Who was it?" I asked.

"A teacher from your school; I don't know who. All Americans look the same to me."

"Did she say anything?"

"She said she knew you. She asked if I was your mother. She said you aren't stupid, but you misuse your talent."

—

"You have too much of your mother in you," my father said to me later. "You need to be more of a man. Get your gear."

I put on boots and a rain jacket and picked up my fishing tools.

My father took me at night to the edge of a swamp. A wooden rowboat was sitting in the grass next to the water.

We climbed into the boat and shoved off. The swamp was large; I couldn't see its boundaries. Around us, trunks of dead trees stuck up through the water. I could imagine an alternate world existing in the darkness, a world of unearthly beings and odd rituals.

The boat had a slow leak, and after some minutes water covered the bottom of the hull. My father gave me a tin can and said, "Start bailing."

I scooped water and threw it over the side repeatedly, but I never caught up with the leak. The water level fell slowly, then rose when I stopped. We placed our feet outside the puddle.

My father threw pieces of cheese into the water to attract fish. He held a flashlight as we baited our hooks and cast our lines. Bobbers had been clipped to the lines, and now and then my father shone his light on the red-and-white floats. Otherwise, all I could see was black water and tree trunks, outlined by the dull glow of the night sky. The water smelled like rotting leaves. Strange creatures could be living in the swamp, creatures as unwholesome as the decaying vegetation.

After a while, rain started, but we didn't row back to shore.

Once or twice, a fish bit. At the end of our outing, we had a couple of bullhead catfish in a bucket. The fish could breathe out of water, and when we got home they were still alive.

My father showed me how to clean the fish. "Don't grab their spines," he said. "The venom will poison you."

He held a fish behind its gills and made two cuts on the side of its head, then used pliers to pull the skin off. Even without skin, the fish flipped in my father's hand. "You don't need to behead them," he said.

He filleted the meat from the sides of the fish and cut off the top fins. He threw the rest of the carcass away.

"Maybe this will make you less of a Nancy," he said.

My mother cooked the fish. "I'm making them the traditional Chinese way," she said, "though I hardly remember how."

The smell of ginger filled the air.

—

The next time I went to chop weeds at the farm, I dug up some burdock roots and put them into a bag. I stripped off some burdock leaves and kept them, too. I brought the plant parts home, put them into a pot with water, and boiled the concoction on the stove.

When my mother saw what I was doing, she said, "The smell reminds me of the herbal shops where I grew up. They had bags and barrels of magical things. There was an herbal cure for every disease, even cancer."

I didn't tell her why I wanted my "tea." I let the water boil down until the mixture was strong. I filled a glass and drank the liquid. It tasted bitter, and faintly of manure. I waited to see if my perceptions would be altered. I looked around to see if colors were intensified. I wondered if people would look like animals.

My mother was working at the sink. "The steam helps my throat," she said. "When I was child and had a cold, I would drink tea and listen to Buddhist monks chanting in the hills."

I went to my room and stared at a light bulb. I wanted to reach to the other side of the light. I wanted to put out my hand and find the source of energy. But I didn't see any higher power in the brightness. I didn't see whoever the Creator was.

All the light did was hurt my eyes. It might have damaged my retinas, burned scars into the backs of my eyeballs. I saw dark spots and strings floating across my field of vision. When I blinked, the specks disappeared. When I blinked again, the motes returned. I looked around as dark amoebas floated through the air.

Safe Colors

FOLLOWING MY FATHER'S INSTRUCTIONS, I PUT ON bright-colored clothing before going into the woods. I pulled on an orange leather hat—it had a bill and earflaps. I didn't like the way it fit. The hat was too thin—it wouldn't be warm enough—but I wore it anyway.

I rode with my father as he drove on a dirt track between fields and parked at the edge of trees. "People go crazy during hunting season," he told me. "They shoot doe instead of bucks. They shoot cows instead of deer. They shoot people, too. A man sitting on a log got shot because he looked like a turkey."

"But don't worry," my father added. "If someone shoots at you, just jump up and wave your arms."

I walked carefully in my blaze-orange hat. Whenever I heard a shot, I expected a bullet to come my way. I was ready to jump up, flail my arms, and yell, "Don't shoot! I'm a person!"

In school, I went to a meeting of a club that promoted international relations. There was only one other student in the meeting: a girl with glasses and hair trimmed at the shoulder. She told me the purpose of the club was to prepare for a student conference that would duplicate a United Nations session. We had been assigned the country of Pakistan. "It's a good country for you," she said, "because you look Punjabi."

She added that since there were only two of us, we would both be ambassadors.

"What does 'ambassadors' mean?" I asked.

"It means we can speak in the General Assembly."

"What will we speak about?"

"Anything we want. We'll have to write a resolution."

———

At home, I watched television with my brother and sister. My sister lay on the floor while my brother stood in a doorway. We followed detectives as they tracked a kidnapper. Oddly, the kidnapper was played by young man who, in real life, was a member of a boy band. In the show, he wasn't entertaining anyone. He was keeping a young woman in a wire cage.

I didn't believe the character. I saw the young man as a pop singer. The woman in the cage seemed distressed, however.

When the detectives found the perpetrator, I wasn't totally glad they did. The kidnapper was arrested before he had a chance to sing.

When I got into bed, my mother surprised me by coming into my room. She crouched next to my bed and said quietly, "Your first word was *gun*."

I remembered a silver-colored six-shooter that I'd carried in a holster. The pistol had the parts of a handgun, but all it shot was caps. When the trigger was pulled, there was a sharp report, but nothing came out of the barrel. I still owned that pistol, but I didn't know where it was.

"Your father likes guns," my mother said. "But we didn't have guns where I grew up. My father was a pacifist, teaching the Christian way in China."

"Where is he now?" I asked.

"I don't know. He was rounded up as a counterrevolutionary."

⌒

The girl in the international-relations club came to visit me. She wanted to prepare for our conference. "Do you have any ideas for a resolution?" she asked me. "You should know about the East."

I hadn't thought about a resolution. All I knew was that the East was Red. My bright idea was to take a gun outside and fire it. "I'll show you how to shoot," I said.

I picked up a deer rifle and some cartridges and led my classmate up a hill behind the town. When we came to a flat, open area, I handed her the gun.

"It has a hair trigger," I said. "When you take off the safety, all you have to do is touch the lever."

She was holding the gun at her side. I was standing next to her, and the gun was between us. Somehow, she released the safety and put her finger on the trigger, and the gun went off. A slug from the rifle could cut through brush and drop a deer at a range of a hundred yards. It was a jungle-hunting gun. The blast shocked me, and it must have frightened my companion, too. Luckily, the gun had been pointed at the ground.

"You have to aim first," I said. "You have to lift the gun to your shoulder and sight down the barrel. Then you breathe out so your hand doesn't shake, and touch off the shot."

"I don't want to shoot anymore," she said.

She went home without working on the school project with me.

⌒

I found the toy pistol I'd played with as a toddler. It had been stored in a box. The gun had a chamber that held caps on a roll of red paper. I put the gun in a holster and buckled the belt around my waist.

I stood in front of a mirror and practiced my draw. In a duel, the gunman who drew faster would shoot first and kill his opponent—unless he missed. I wanted to fire and hit. I wanted to survive. After a number of tries, I quickened my draw. I might not have been the fastest gunman, but I was the fastest gun boy.

—

I prepared a resolution for the international relations club. In the paper, I asked neighboring countries to support Pakistan's new government. I didn't think India and Afghanistan would vote for my proposal—they were my rivals—but I might get votes from the superpowers. A couple of them wanted Pakistan on the Security Council. I looked forward to speaking in front of the General Assembly.

When I showed my proposal to the girl in my delegation, she said, "I can see you worked hard on this, but I'm quitting the club."

I decided to go to the conference on my own. I would be a delegation of one.

—

The night before I was to leave for the U.N. meeting, I had a dream about my family. My brother and sister and I were going hunting with my father. But we didn't head for the woods or the countryside. We went to a town that had been remodeled as a tourist attraction. An orchestra was playing in an open area. All of the buildings were newly restored.

Our father led us into a renovated structure—its old storefront was now a gift shop—but I wanted to leave it and walk out to the fields. I could see grassland through the windows. I walked to the back, but there was no exit.

I was wearing a green jacket, and I knew green was not a safe color to wear in the woods. My brother and sister were also wearing green jackets. No one had a bright-colored article of clothing. Any one of us could have been shot by mistake.

Holding the Gun

M Y FATHER BROUGHT OUT A HANDGUN: A BLACK SERVICE revolver that fit easily into the palm of his hand. "I got this from my father," he said. "He used to keep it at the bank.

"It's hammerless," he added. "You just pull the trigger."

He demonstrated by holding the gun at arm's length and pointing the muzzle at the floor. The chamber rotated as he squeezed the trigger, and the firing pin clicked.

"The problem is, the barrel moves when you pull the trigger, so you can't aim. Someone would have to be very close for you to hit him."

I pictured a banker—my grandfather—holding the gun and firing rapidly at an intruder. The criminal would be wearing a bandanna over his face and would be clutching a bag of cash. He would bob and weave as he ran for the door. Behind him, the suited banker would be spraying bullets into the surrounding air.

"Was the bank ever robbed?" my mother asked.

"No," my father said.

⁓

I turned on the television and watched a show about a professional burglar. This man was named after a gun maker,

Remington. He had switched sides and now enforced the law. He didn't wear a bandanna over his face, and in fact the camera often zoomed in on his stern facial features.

In the current episode, Remington was using his skills to break into an art museum. Laser beams laced the passageway to an inner room. In his black catsuit, Remington slithered under the shafts of light to reach the prize: an object in a glass case.

Not surprisingly, Remington had a girlfriend, a woman who had never been a criminal. She had always been a straight-arrow type and now owned a sleuthing company. She was Remington's boss. He would not "break and enter" unless she told him to do so.

I had to stop watching the show when my father came home from the local bar. "The rich get richer," he announced to no one, "and the poor get poorer."

My mother heard him and said, "We should be grateful for what we have."

"We'll have more," my father said, "when we take the wealth and redistribute it."

"'I was complaining I had no shoes until I met a man who had no feet.'" my mother said. "That's what I learned as a child."

"I've had enough of your Confucianism," my father said. "It's more like *Confusionism*. This is America, not China. We'll take from the rich and give to the poor. I don't care if it means robbing a bank."

—

I picked up the revolver and spun the cylinder. I tested my ability to aim the gun by holding it at arm's length and squeezing the trigger. I wanted to keep the barrel steady when the internal hammer snapped forward. But the pressure of my finger on the trigger pulled the barrel slightly to the right. I considered aiming a bit to the left, but how would I know how far to the left? It made no sense to aim off the target in order to hit the target. I figured I should just fire as many times as possible. That would stop whoever was coming at me.

My father lined up his new artworks on the floor and called me to look at them. The paintings showed a huddled female figure in different landscapes. I recognized the landscapes as scenes outside our windows: farm fields in the foreground, wooded hills in the background.

I looked at the images and said nothing.

"Don't you have anything to say?" my father asked.

I didn't reply.

"Nobody cares what I do," he said. "The problem is, I have children, and I can't pay for children. We're going to change our lifestyle. We're going to live off the land. We're going to stake a claim and grow our own food."

He pointed with a finger. "Go out and clear the land."

I walked to our backyard and looked at the patch of ground where our father would plant a garden. The growing season in this part of Appalachia hadn't started yet, so the earth was bare. I picked up some fist-sized pebbles and set them on the border of the potential garden.

A groundhog ambled into the yard and poked around. The animal was in the open when my father appeared with his handgun. He fired one shot, and the rodent sat up. It tucked its forelegs under its chin and stared with weak eyes in the direction of the report, then moved off to safety.

"There went our dinner," my father said.

My brother and I decided to go camping, but we weren't ambitious enough to walk to the woods. We pitched our pup tent in our backyard.

Our tent could hold two people. We could lie in it, but we couldn't stretch our arms or legs. We had sleeping bags, but no cushions. We lay like mummies—arms crossed over our chest—on the hard ground. After dark, the air became cold, and moisture collected on every surface. We shivered in our down-filled bags.

We heard a rustling outside. "What's that?" I asked.

"The wind," my brother said, "or leaves blown by the wind."

"No. It's an animal, or a ghost."

"It's a cat, or the ghost of a cat."

I was sure the ghost was human. I pictured an ectoplasmic female figure in a white gown floating over the lawn. The figure made no sounds—no screams or moans—but her gown flapped in the wind.

We lay in silence for a while. Then we ran from the tent and into the house. My brother headed for the room he shared with our sister, and I went to the room I occupied alone.

The next time my father returned from the bar, he seemed to be having trouble walking. He steadied himself against the kitchen stove.

"The sheriff can't keep us down," he said. "I've got a band of merry men, and we're going to take over. But first we'll go to the mead hall, listen to the bard, and drink some honey wine."

"We had opium eaters where I grew up," my mother said. "But we rebelled against the gangsters who were making us sleep all the time."

"I don't care about your Boxers or your kickboxers. Our ruling dynasty lives in Washington. That's where we're going."

My father left the house to meet his joyful men.

⁓

I looked for the service revolver but couldn't find it. I remembered it was kept in a valise, the kind a burglar like Remington would carry. But the case wasn't where it was supposed to be. I moved furniture and boxes. I cleared a space down to the floor, but I didn't see the gun. I wanted the weapon, if not to shoot it, at least to hold it, to feel its power in my hand.

⁓

I picked up a record album and looked at its cover. On the back was a puzzle. The idea was to trace a path through a maze and get to the center. The words "IT'S HERE!" were printed in psychedelic lettering in the middle of the maze. Using a fingertip, I entered the doorway and wound my way through the passages. Presently, I hit a blockade. There was no way around it. The artist had designed the maze so it could not be navigated. It resembled an ancient king's labyrinth, where no one could find safety before being torn apart by the Minotaur.

I searched again for the handgun but couldn't find it.

"It's Here!"

I HEARD THE SOUND OF FARAWAY THUNDER, BUT THE NOISE could have come from something falling, something hitting the floor. I tried to ignore the sound, but it was persistent.

When the sky claps came closer, my father set up chairs on our front porch so we could watch the storm. I sat next to him, and we looked and listened as lightning preceded thunder at shorter and shorter intervals.

"Is it the end of the world?" my father asked. "I don't mean the climate or the weather. I mean the collapse of everything."

I couldn't see much. All I saw was a dark-gray wall of rain; I couldn't see the hill that bordered the valley. Large drops blew in under the porch roof and onto my face.

My father picked up a beer bottle and said, "The Republicans are grasping pieces of flotsam in the flood. The Democrats are underwater. They're holding their noses and sending up air bubbles."

I watched the rain bouncing off the blacktop of the street. I didn't move from my seat as the storm went on.

"Who will stop it?" my father asked. "No one."

⁓

Inside, I picked up a record album and looked at the back cover. I had studied this cover many times. There was a labyrinth on the square ground—I knew there was no way through it. I saw the words "IT'S HERE!" in the middle of the maze, but I didn't pick up a pencil or pen to trace a path. Instead, I looked at the cover of the album, photographed in 3-D. When I tilted the cover, the faces of the band members turned. They were sitting in a garden of red and yellow flowers, and behind them the Alps rose. A temple stood in the middle of the mountains. In the sky, very close to Earth, was a red Saturn. The idea seemed to be that you could not get to where "IT" was, but you could listen to the record, at high volume, anytime.

⁓

When my father saw me sitting, he said, "Get up! When I was in the Army we woke at sunrise and marched all day. We covered fifty miles with gear on our backs. We didn't stop until we were about to die."

I stood and went out to the front porch. In front of me was the old main route, now a small street, and now clear of cars. I heard a knocking and looked over the railing. My brother and sister were pounding on something below. I stepped down to join them.

"I won't walk on the porch," my sister said. "There's something under there. I can't see it, but I know it's there."

"Are you sure?" I asked.

My sister had had trouble seeing from an early age. Once, my father told me to cover one eye with a hand and try to get around that way. "That's how your sister sees," he'd said. "She has a lazy eye."

She and my brother continued to tear at the lattice between the porch floor and the ground. They used their hands to pull slats apart. I looked at the space they had opened but saw nothing beyond the bare dirt.

"When this screen is gone," my sister said, "the thing will have nothing to hide behind. I'll see it then."

⁓

I walked past my father's unheated studio, and when he noticed me, he called me in.

"I'm making silk-screen prints of butterflies," he said, and held up a sample.

He had created a perfect swallowtail, rendered to scale and in real-life colors, on a piece of gray paper.

"Butterflies are disappearing," he added. "We used to see clouds of butterflies in the fields. Now, you might see one or two."

I could picture those yellow and white sulfur butterflies swarming over puddles of water.

"I'm going to make lots of these prints and sell them cheaply," my father said. "Anyone can have a work of art for five dollars."

⁓

My father took my siblings and me to an art fair in the neighboring college town. He had rented a display table on a downtown street.

"I'm going to give a silk-screening presentation," he said. "I'll show how I make prints, and then I'll sell them."

My brother and sister and I walked to the end of the street, to where a stage had been set up. A band called Beowulf and the Geats was playing. The songs were loud and, in my opinion, totally satisfying. The Geats looked suitably fierce. My siblings and I listened in awe to an entire set.

When we got back to my father's table, we saw prints of butterflies hanging on a clothesline. The paper sheets were attached with wooden pins. "These prints are drying," my father said. "You don't have to be a collector to buy one. You can be anyone."

∿

In a record store, I looked for albums by Beowulf and the Geats but couldn't find any, so I asked a clerk about the band.

"Do you mean Beowulf and the Goths?" he asked.

"No, the Geats. You know, from Sweden."

"The Visigoths?"

"The Geats."

"Never heard of them," he said.

∿

In the evening, I watched a TV show with my brother and sister. At one point, I looked through the living-room window and saw a soldier on the porch. He was marching in one direction, then the other, lifting his elbows and his knees high. The figure could have been a reflection of a man on the TV screen, the result of a convergence of light rays that formed a hologram. But there was no such figure on the TV screen.

I pointed so that all of us could see.

"He came from under the porch," my sister said. "We opened the way."

∿

Later, I picked up the album cover with the maze on the back and found a sharp knife. With the blade, I scratched out the line that blocked me from getting to the center. With the line gone, I could easily trace a path through the tangled corridors to the words "IT'S HERE!"

New Age

AT DINNER, AS USUAL, MY FATHER SPOKE WHILE THE REST of my family listened. "I'm tired of being poor," he began, "and I'm only getting poorer."

No one responded, but my brother and sister and I tried to eat. My mother stood at a distance.

"The banks have money," my father continued, "because we give it to them. If everyone took their money out, the banks would go broke. I have no money in the bank and none in my pocket. Well, I might have a nickel, but I don't have a second one to rub against it. I don't have enough for a drink."

"I support this family," my mother said.

"She works," my father said. "She's liberated."

My brother, sister and I stopped eating and left the kitchen. My mother stayed, and I could hear my father complaining to her about finances.

~

I wanted to make my own money. I had seen a print ad that promised cash rewards for carrying newspapers. A delivery boy could make enough to buy a bicycle. The problem was, another boy already had the local paper route. There were about thirty houses in our town, and almost all of them subscribed to the paper, so there were no other potential customers.

I asked the boy if I could share his route, and he said I could substitute when he was unable to deliver.

"How often would that be?" I asked.

"Maybe once a month."

At that rate, I figured, it would take me several years to earn enough to buy a bicycle. Still, I took my substitute day and walked the length of the town—about a mile one way—to deliver papers. A couple of customers owned dogs that bared their teeth and chased me, but I finished the route unharmed.

—

As soon as I got a ride to the nearby college town, I visited a store called People's Nation. The place sold many "alternative" items: suede bell-bottoms, velvet jackets, skinny jeans, rolling papers, incense sticks, and books on counterculture. I had a few dollars in my pocket for shopping.

I leafed through a book that contained lyrics to a song I'd heard but could never understand. The song revealed that a fire had hit a town. Not only were the streets burning, but a mad bull was running loose. I didn't know if the lyrics were poetry, but I was alarmed. You didn't want to be on the streets when they were on fire and a crazy animal was charging. I couldn't afford the book, so I tried to memorize the lyrics.

A package of incense cost less than a dollar. I bought a long, narrow envelope that held a few sticks. I also bought a book about spiritual enlightenment, written by a former Harvard professor who had become a servant of God.

At home, I had no incense burner: no metal stand, ceramic bowl, or wooden tray. All I had was a piece of rubber that I used as an eraser. I molded the wad around the end of the incense stick and propped it on my desk.

I picked up the new book. The dark-blue cover was scored with geometric lines, and the text urged me not to remain a caterpillar, but to become a butterfly. I would learn to trust, to love. I would become an illuminated being, like the author, who had achieved enlightenment by taking LSD when it was legal.

I lit the incense stick and put my nose over the tip. The smoke stung my nostrils and concealed any fragrance the incense might have had.

My father brought home a bag of oysters out of the shell. When my mother saw the gray mass of mollusks, she said, "Oysters are dangerous. You can get very sick."

My father turned the plastic bag in his hands, as if inspecting each body. "They look fine," he said.

My father breaded the oysters and fried them. He stacked them on a platter and spooned some onto plates. I took a plate and started to eat. I didn't care for the oysters themselves, but the browned crust was good.

While we were eating, my father said, "We should make a run on the banks. We should take out all our money, and everyone else should do the same."

"We don't have money to take out," my mother said.

"We'll shut down the banks!" my father shouted.

My mother fetched her pocketbook and found a bill. "Take this," she said.

"May we be excused?" I asked.

"Yes, go!"

Hours later, the oysters hadn't made me sick, but I had a queasy feeling from my father's conversation.

—

I lit a match and sucked on the mouthpiece of one of my father's pipes. He had a couple of dozen that he stored on a rack: a corncob, a clay, a meerschaum, and several brier-woods. The goo left from burned tobacco coated their bowls and stems. It didn't matter which pipe I sampled; I could inhale the heated tar residue. The taste was foul, but the substance seemed to have a kick, as if the nicotine was active. Of course, it would have been better to smoke fresh tobacco, to take a chunk from a pouch, tamp it into a bowl, and fire it up. But doing that would have revealed the secret that I was a tobacco addict.

—

My father brought me outside to work in his garden. He had sown lettuce seeds close together, and my task was to make more room for the plants. "Pull them out by the roots," my father said.

I did as I was told. The lettuce had substantial anchors for such small plants—they were stuck fast to the dirt.

"And throw them on the ground."

I went along a row, pulling and tossing the smaller plants.

"We're going to live on the food in this garden," my father said. "We're going to live like animals in nature. Do you see any sick rabbits around here?"

I saw no rabbits at all.

—

I went to my room and lit a stick of incense. I was careful not to put my nose too close to the smoke—I had learned from the mystic's book not to trust completely. I took a pinch of tobacco I'd stolen from my father's workroom and put it in a pipe I'd made from aluminum foil. The pipe was wrinkled and flimsy, but it was somewhat airtight, and when I inhaled, smoke passed through it. I turned on my transistor radio, and in time a DJ played the song about a mad bull running loose. The singer promised that war was not far away, but love was not far away, either.

Questionable Moves

I WAS LOOKING AT MY FATHER'S BOOKSHELVES WHEN I noticed things other than books. My father had put ceramics in the empty spaces. There were some vases and bowls, but among the ordinary objects were two figures. They were made from red clay, maybe terra-cotta, and their surfaces were rough—each stood about a foot-and-a-half tall. They were wearing robes, so their arms and legs were hidden by the folds of the "cloth." Their faces were simplified, yet suggested nobility. Each was wearing a crown: They were a king and queen.

It wasn't clear if they were a specific king and queen, or whether they were generic. But after some thought, I realized they were chess pieces. I didn't see a giant chessboard or any other outsize pieces to match. Maybe my father hadn't planned for these objects to be used in an actual game of chess. They were as heavy as rocks, and anyone playing with them would have a hard time making moves. I lifted the two objects and set them on the floor, turning them to face each other. I didn't know who they were supposed to represent. They could have been modeled after specific historical figures, or after my parents.

I pictured thirty-two pieces like the ones I'd found. Would players have to climb ladders to see patterns on the chess-board? Would they have to climb down, lug a piece across squares, and ascend again to contemplate their next move? The question was not important, since no pieces other than the king and queen existed.

—

When he got home from the local bar, my father complained to my mother about my siblings and me. "They are not my children. They are your children. They are Chinese children."

"They are American," my mother said

"That's the problem!" my father shouted. "I moved here to live apart from society, but they are ordinary Americans."

"How so?"

"They want things."

"But we don't have things."

"That's what I'm saying! We have no things to give them!"

—

My siblings and I went to the playground at the nearby school. The area was usually empty, but on this day we arrived to find an adult. He had dark hair, a trimmed beard, and a tidy mustache. He was working as the playground's instructor. He was waiting for other children to come, but none did.

My brother and sister wandered around the exercise equipment, and I asked the instructor what I could do.

"Do you play chess?" he asked.

I knew how to play, but I was impatient. I didn't want to spend time thinking about my moves. I wanted to see the pattern on the board and get a feeling of the game. I wanted to think only one move ahead, but I wanted it to be the right move.

"Yes," I said.

The instructor and I sat a small table outside the school building, under a half roof. I had the white pieces; my first move was pawn to king four.

"Are you sandbagging me?" my opponent asked as he also moved his pawn to king four.

I wasn't sure what he meant, but I knew my move was Bobby Fischer's standard opening.

The game began competitively, but my position quickly worsened. My decision to castle did not protect my king. My opponent swatted my pawns aside and leaped over my moat with a horse. I looked to a bishop for comfort, but he couldn't offer a prayer. My queen was my only hope, and she desperately ran one way and another, across the length of the board.

The black side, on the other hand, made no mistakes. He ensconced his king in a strong fortress, with towers at two corners, and used a heavily armed knight to protect the entrance. His pawns advanced steadily toward promotion, as his bishops' prayers were answered. His queen was wise, working behind the scenes to support his army. I didn't have a chance.

⌣

I wanted to join a chess club at school, but I quickly learned that my school had no such club. The closest thing was a math club, so I went to the first meeting of that group. The gathering was held in an empty classroom after school hours. When I arrived, I saw only a few other students, all boys. No one seemed to be in charge, and there was no agenda for discussion. We sat at desks, behind the curved writing arms, and looked at each other.

"We could discuss quadratic equations," one student said.

"What are quadratic equations?" I asked.

"Well, they have a squared variable in them."

"They sound like they're for squares," another student said.

"Are we squares?" I asked.

"I'm not a square."

At the end of our discussion, we did not schedule another meeting.

—

I found a tray of broken glass among my father's art materials. The fragments were of different colors, and the primary hues were intense. I picked out some of the pieces and tried to fit them together, but I couldn't form a recognizable shape.

When my father saw me handling the glass, he said, "You have to cut the pieces to size." He picked up a tool with a sharp wheel on one end, laid a straightedge along a pane, and scored the glass with one stroke. He aligned the score mark with the side of a table and snapped the glass with his free hand. "Do it fast," he explained.

Using the same method, I tried cutting a piece of glass myself. The glass broke, but not where I had wanted. It came apart in a curved line, roughly at right angles to my score.

"Practice," my father said, "until you have the touch."

He showed me a drawing of a Biblical scene, with dark lines separating each piece of color. "I designed this window for a church. It's there now, in the front wall. We could go to see it, but it's far away."

I pictured the sketch blown up to the size of a two-story building, with light coming through the panes.

"I started with ceramics," my father said, "then worked for a stained-glass company. But I lost that job over politics."

"How?" I asked.

"I didn't like a presidential candidate, and I said so. My bosses thought I was going to assassinate him."

"What happened?"

"I moved my family here, to nowhere. We went from somewhere to nowhere. Now, I make my own art prints. If anyone wants one, they can buy it for next to nothing. And if they can't afford that, I'll give it to them."

—

At school, I took a shop class in ceramics. The assignment was to make a coil pot, glaze it, and fire it in a kiln.

We rolled wet clay into ropes with our palms. Then we cut the strands into lengths. For the base of the pot, we wrapped a strand into a disk shape, then built the vessel by winding clay strands upward. We let the clay dry, then added glaze. I painted the inside of my vase white and the outside black. The piece stood about three inches high. I fired it in a kiln, then brought it home as a gift for my parents.

"What will we do with it?" my mother asked.

"You can put flowers in it."

"Very small ones," she said.

"Anyone can make art," my father said, "but hardly anyone can make good art."

I set the vase on my father's bookshelf, next to the ceramic king and queen.

—

My mother made an origami bird by folding a piece of paper. She held the bird by its body and pulled on its tail, and its wings flapped. She handed it to me, and I did the same. I pulled on the tail, then let go. The wings folded down, then unfolded straight out. "What kind of bird is it?" I asked.

"It's a crane," she said. "It has a long neck and long pointed wings. In China, it stands for nobility and longevity, as well as lasting love."

"Shouldn't it have long legs, too?"

"This one has no legs."

⸻

I found a worn-out paperback titled *Chess Strategies* on my father's shelf. I paged through the book and found the Ruy Lopez opening, the Caro-Kann defense, and the Nimzo-Indian defense. I glanced at the king's gambit and the queen's gambit. I noticed strategies for open boards and others for central domination. None of it meant anything to me, but I thought I could slowly memorize sequences of moves. If I became sidetracked or bored, I could switch to origami. I could always manage the folding of paper.

Making Plays

MY FATHER WOULDN'T ALLOW MY SIBLINGS AND ME TO watch football games on television. He disapproved of the sport; to him it seemed like combat, a display of brute force. He didn't see any grace in the players' moves—he saw no ballet in running, passing, or catching.

My sister wasn't interested in football, so it was no loss for her not to watch it on TV. But I understood the game and found it exciting. I liked seeing the attacking players move the ball forward, yard by yard. I appreciated the acrobatic tackles, where the ball carrier would be upended in a no-hands cartwheel in the air.

The no-football rule was hardest for my brother, who played football at our high school. He was good at running and jumping—he brought those skills to the game. Mainly, he was fast, so he trained as a defensive back. His task was to swat the ball away from opposing receivers, make tackles, and intercept passes.

To discourage my brother from playing, my father wouldn't give him a ride to football practice. My mother worked all day and couldn't take him, either. So my brother rode his bicycle to the field. The trip was ten miles in one direction—"a workout in itself," my brother said.

⁓

One time, I asked him what he had done at practice.

"We learned how to tackle," he said.

"Do you aim for the knees with your arms?" I asked.

"No," he said. "We bring our fist down on the back of a guy's helmet before he leaves the line of scrimmage."

He made a motion to show how he would punch the back of someone's head.

"Is that a tackle?" I asked.

"It flattens the guy before he starts to run."

My brother was younger than I was, but he was bigger and stronger. His fist-to-helmet move impressed me.

⁓

My father took me to a bookstore in the nearby college town. He showed me a display of coffee mugs, T-shirts, and framed prints featuring the university's mascot, a mountain lion. "I did the artwork for these," he said.

I looked closely at the images. The contours and shading defined shape and volume, yet were not photographic. The drawings were works of art.

My father wandered around the store and found a large-format book that contained color plates of tropical butterflies. "I'll buy this with my freelance money," he said.

As we walked past a display area, we saw a poster that looked like an advertisement for the movie *Jaws*. But instead of showing the word "Jaws," the headline read "Joe's." The first name of the university's football coach was Joe. The players were Joe's team. They were strong and fierce, like sharks, and they performed for Joe. On Joe's orders, they would tear apart and swallow any opponent.

"I like that idea," my father said.

⏝

I stole some tobacco from a can in my father's studio and rolled a cigarette using a glue-strip paper. My cigarette was lumpy—fat in the middle but thin at the ends. It looked like a pregnant snake. I took it to my bedroom and smoked it. I thought no one would see me there.

Presently, my brother said to me, "I know you're smoking the old man's tobacco."

"I'd smoke stronger stuff," I said, "but I don't have any."

"I'll show you something," he said.

He led me to the top of the nearby ridge. We rode our bicycles uphill, walked the last steep stretch, and parked on a gravel pull-off. We hiked into the woods, staying on the top of the hill line as we went. When we came to a clearing, my brother pointed out several plants with palmate leaves. "I dropped some seeds here," he said. "They're growing fast."

"I didn't know you had seeds," I said.

"That's all I had."

The plants stood on a patch of cleared earth. They looked healthy—lush and bright green. Who knew if they would be potent? In our part of Appalachia, the soil was loamy, the days rainy. We didn't have the sandy soil and sunny climate that would support ten-foot marijuana stalks with lots of flowers.

⏝

At dinner, my father asked my mother for money. "I just need a few dollars," he said.

"Why don't you use your own money?" she asked. "You made prints for the university."

"I bought a butterfly book," he said. "It was expensive."

"I support this family."

"You don't support me," he said. "If I need money, I'll get it."

She handed him a bill, and he pocketed it. Later, I noticed he was gone. I didn't have to ask where he was. No one had to ask. Everyone knew he was at the local bar, probably sitting alone, drinking until he was ready to come home. All of us hoped he would be quiet when he arrived.

⁓

My brother gave me some leaves from his plants on the hill. "Smoke 'em if you got 'em," he said.

I waited a couple of days, then rolled the dried leaves in a cigarette paper and lit the stick. The smoke was sharp, like fumes from a burning lawn, without much fragrance.

I turned on the television and saw a man threatened with death. I thought the man was a goner. A bad guy was pointing a machine gun at him. The hero happened to be the captain of a starship. I knew the show was a fantasy, but I saw no way out for the captain. Yet I knew that, since the captain was a recurring character, he would not be killed. He would get his own machine gun. If that didn't work, he would use his phaser, which was more powerful than a machine gun. Beyond that, his first officer could use his nerve pinch to subdue attackers. If all else failed, an engineer on the orbiting starship could beam him up.

I couldn't believe any of it. The action was ridiculous. Everyone should have died.

⁓

My father called me to his studio, where he was sitting at his drafting table under a fluorescent desk light. "You're going to leave here soon," he said. "What are you going to do?"

"I'll apply to college," I said.

"You need life experience, not college. You should get a van and live in it."

"What kind of van?"

"A vw bus, painted like a hippie-mobile."

"I want to apply to college," I said.

"OK, but when you go to an interview, tell them what you think. If they ask what you'd do to improve your high school, say you'd get rid of football."

"Why?"

"If you want football, join the Army."

—

I stayed after school to go to a football game—the rest of my family didn't show up.

My brother was playing defense for the home team. The opposing players were from a larger, richer school, the one in the college town. They quickly took the lead and held it.

On one play, my brother chased a pass from the other team. He was on the far side of the field and running toward me. He caught the ball and returned it for a number of yards.

I called his name from the bleachers, and my voice carried across the stadium. "Rutkowski!" I yelled.

He turned his head when he heard me but couldn't find me in the bleachers. I knew he'd heard my call. He knew I was there to support him.

After the game, my brother stayed with his team, and someone from the stands gave me a ride home. I was filled with the story of the pass interception. I looked forward to telling the rest of my family about the pick. It was the game's best play.

Through the Air

A FRIEND OF MY FATHER'S CAME TO VISIT. YEARS EARLIER, this same friend had traveled to our house in the country. He was someone from Somewhere. Since then, he'd gotten a teaching job at an upstate university. When I next saw him, he looked the same: like a beatnik, with a beard and mustache. He was sitting in the kitchen with my father. They were drinking beer from mugs and ignoring the black-and-white television, which was playing silently.

"How long did it take you to get here?" my father asked.

"About an hour."

"How did you do that? It would take me four or five hours," my father said.

"I flew in a straight line, in my plane," the friend said. "I landed at the local airport and picked up a car."

My father invited me to join them and poured another glass of beer. I sat at the table and took a sip—the liquid was strong and bitter. I set the glass in front of me and looked at it instead of at the men.

The friend was talking about his aerial art. "My work is an extension of Futurism," he explained. "The Futurists wanted speed, and they used technology. They found both with airplanes."

He demonstrated with a fork and an empty beer mug. "I go straight up with the engine on full blast." He lifted his device and made roaring sounds in his throat.

"Then the engine stalls out." He turned the fork and mug over and lowered them toward the floor. He rattled the fork inside the mug to approximate a coughing motor. "I restart it before I hit the ground."

"How do you show your art?" my father asked.

"I make smoke trails while I fly, and someone on the ground takes photos. I use the photos, along with prints of my wing patterns, to make collages. I write words like 'Roaaarrr' over the images."

—

When the friend left the room, my father said to me. "I'm no Futurist. The Futurists couldn't see what was going to happen. Where will they be tomorrow?"

He rolled a cigarette, licked the paper and pulled crumbs of tobacco off his lips. "I look to the past; I look for what we've lost. No one cares about what I do."

He brought me to his studio and gestured toward an old tricycle on the floor. "See that?" he said.

There were no colors on the warped object, and the surface was uniformly brown. The wheels and pedals were frozen with rust.

"I found that in a field," he said. "I'm going to make paintings of it, just as soon as I get the time. Now, I have to spend all of my time with you kids. You don't know what to do with yourselves."

I went to find my brother and sister so we could do something on our own. We walked out to the yard, paced the edges of the grass, then walked back in. We sat in our rooms.

When my father's friend offered to take my siblings and me for a ride, we became excited. Our father didn't like body-tossing rides, so he didn't go along.

At the airfield, the pilot led me across the tarmac to his plane. "It's a Citabria," he said. "That's 'Airbatic' spelled backwards."

I got into the plane's back seat. In front of me, the pilot walked to the propeller and grabbed it with both hands. He rotated the blade a couple of times, then got into his seat and adjusted some knobs. He stepped out and swung the propeller again. The engine caught, and the propeller became a blur.

"Do we have parachutes?" I asked over the engine's sound.

"No," he shouted. "If anything goes wrong, we'll buy the farm."

As we ascended, I could see the landscape dropping away. The horizon remained steady as we climbed. Suddenly, the horizon vanished and I could see only sky. I felt blood rushing to my head.

"Plus three G's," the pilot announced. "Three gravities."

The horizon came back into view, and the land, with its trees, roads and houses, came toward us.

"Minus two G's."

There was silence as the sky and land slid across the plane's windshield. "The engine stalled," the pilot announced.

I didn't see how he could get out of the plane and restart the motor by spinning the propeller. He pushed a plunger and flipped a switch, and the engine caught. "I had to prime it," he said.

I tapped him on the shoulder and shook my head.

"Had enough?" he said as he leveled the plane.

We took a straight path over a lake and town before heading back to the airfield. I felt better—actually, perfect—as soon as my feet touched the ground.

One after the other, my brother and sister went up in the plane. When they returned, they each said they had enjoyed the flight.

"It was more fun than going to a carnival," my sister said.

"I'd do it again," my brother said.

—

At home, I found my father sitting on the rusted tricycle. He had a beer bottle in one hand and a smoldering cigarette in the other. "I can't get an art show," he said, "because I don't know the technology."

"Maybe you could take a course," I suggested.

"I can't go to school," he said. "I have to take care of you."

He inhaled from the cigarette and drank from the bottle. "I made a mistake," he said. "I should never have had children."

—

After my father's friend had left, my mother said to me, "I asked him not to come back. He makes your father depressed, and then your father treats all of us badly."

"Do you think he'll come back anyway?" I asked.

"He and your father have known each other a long time. You know where they're from. It's a little town. You were there once. Do you remember?"

"I remember being somewhere. I don't remember where."

"I hope he doesn't come back," she said.

"Can I still be friends with him?"

"Maybe he'll get in touch with you, years from now."

—

My father gave me a model kit. With the pieces, I could make a glider out of balsa wood. The parts for the toy were in a plastic bag. I took the slats out and fitted them together. I slid a flat piece through a slot in the fuselage for the wings and pressed strips into smaller slots for the tail fin and stabilizer. I clipped a metal weight onto the nose and took the glider to the yard next to the nearby school. I threw the plane flat out in front of me. The glider arced up, then stalled and came straight down, bouncing when it hit the grass. I adjusted the wings and launched the plane again. It flew up in a gentle arc and landed on the roof of the school building.

I had to climb onto an electrical unit next to the building and jump to the roof. I pulled myself up and swung my legs over. The glider was lying on the gravel that covered the roof. I picked up the aircraft and pitched it from the rim.

Police Truck

W HEN I WAS LEARNING TO DRIVE, THE LAST THING
I wanted to see in my rearview mirror was a police
truck. I knew police officers sometimes used unmarked
vehicles—why not a pickup truck? Sometimes, I would
look into my mirror and see, close behind, a pickup with a
male driver. That person might have been a teenager, like
myself, learning to drive, or he might have been a Smokey
Bear with his hat off. I knew state troopers took their hats
off to look like one of us, to lull us into a false sense of security. As soon as we strayed—bam!—we would be stopped,
arrested, photographed, fingerprinted, probably beaten, and
certainly maimed.

And what of the object on that pickup truck's dashboard?
It could have been a plastic Jesus, or it could have been a radar
gun. The truck driver might have been a Smokey with a speed
detector. He might have been using radio waves to "take my
picture." Or he might have had an actual mechanical camera.
He might have been a Kodiak with a Kodak!

My fear of state troopers echoed my father's paranoia.
Early on, he'd been investigated for planning to assassinate
Richard Nixon. I didn't know if my father was a real threat to

the politician, but the FBI thought he was. Apparently, he'd shot his mouth off in a bar, and word had got back to the feds. My father was required to stay at least fifty miles away from Nixon whenever he came through town. That didn't happen often, because my father had moved his family far from any city shortly after the investigation. Still, he thought our phone was tapped and we should limit what we said. "If you hear a clicking on the line," he warned, "that means the call is being recorded. Don't give out any information; don't say who you are or where you're calling from. And, for God's sake, don't say what you're calling about."

Whenever my father's mother called to say hello, I didn't invite conversation. I didn't say whether my father was in a murderous mood. I answered questions briefly. "This is me," I would say. "Yes, me. ... It's me. ... Fine. ... What? It's me. ... Fine. ... Goodbye."

My father was also suspicious of strangers who came to our door, people such as members of the Jehovah's Witnesses. He was convinced they were government agents. When they tried to give him a copy of *The Watchtower* magazine, he would say, "That's what you do. You sit in your tower and you watch. Who are you looking for? You're looking for me. But I don't have anything against Richard Nixon. I don't even have anything against John Birch. I have a wooden toilet seat. I'm a member of the Birch John Society."

So, when I was learning to drive, I was often aware of being followed. I was looking for trouble, and the road was where to find it. If a friend was riding with me, I would look into my rearview mirror, and if I saw a vehicle on my tail, I would know someone was after me. "Is that a police truck?" I would ask my friend.

My friend would turn and look through the back windshield. "That's no police truck," he would say. "It's a pickup truck, from a farm. I know the guy driving it."

"It's a police truck," I would insist.

Later, when I was home, I would recall the vehicle behind me. The driver might have been a farm boy, or he might have been a Smokey with his hat off. He might have had a radar gun. He might have had a Kodak. He might have already put my picture on the wall of State Police headquarters, so he and his fellow officers could remember what I looked like. The next time they encountered me on the highway, they would know who I was.

part two

The Scientific Method

SHORTLY AFTER I'D FINISHED COLLEGE, I GOT A JOB AT a scientific-texts publisher in New York. I had no background in science, except for a year of biology for nonmajors, but getting the job was easy. All I had to do was pass a spelling test. On a list of words, I identified those I thought were misspelled. I didn't have to spell them correctly; I simply meant I would look them up. On the list were *exponencial, medien, n+1,* and *parabala.*

My new title was production editor, and my salary was less than ten thousand dollars a year. My chums from college might have been surprised at how little I was making, but I kept it to myself. I didn't want anyone to think it was what I was worth.

I was assigned to the journals *General Relativity and Gravitation, Biofeedback and Self-Regulation,* and the *American Journal of Digestive Diseases.* Through my work, I learned about the red shift in electromagnetic radiation, the manipulation of the human body to reduce chronic pain, and people's gastrointestinal health problems. I called the journals GRG, BSR, and AJDD. I had no problem with GRG and BSR, but I thought of AJDD as the *American Journal of Disgusting Diseases.* I found most of the ailments in *AJDD*—especially those illustrated with color photos—distasteful.

⌣

I referred my roommate for a job at the same publisher. I knew him from college, where he'd been an art-history major. We were sharing a loft space near the old seaport downtown; a Japanese artist was subletting the space to us.

I thought my roommate would be a good candidate because he'd written many research papers. He understood scholarship. But he was not offered a spot at the publisher. After he'd left the office, the woman who'd given him the entrance test told me, "He's a nice guy, but he can't spell."

⌣

At night, my roommate and I went to visit our next-door neighbor, the Japanese artist. He was a sculptor, but his main job was carpentry. He was building a large cube for a well-known Conceptualist; the cube conformed to precise measurements for the length of each edge and the arc of each angle. The instructions would be exhibited along with the finished object. Using the directions, anyone could make a cube of their own.

We sat at the "kitchen" table in our neighbor's loft and got loaded on weed. After we were jacked, we played with the artist's .22-caliber pistol. We pointed it at each other and laughed uncontrollably. At one point, the artist took the gun, raised it to shoulder level, and fired across the room. A couple of telephone books were stacked against the wall, and they flew from the hit. He walked across the room and picked up the books. "Look at how the bullet went through both," he said.

At a certain hour, I jumped up from the table. "I have to go to work in the morning," I said.

"You are never late," the artist said.

⁓

In the office, my task was to prepare equations in type-script for a printer. I had to underline each variable so it would be set in italics. This was easy with x, y, and z, but I was puzzled by the characters for alpha, epsilon, and sigma. I had to seek assistance for those. Then I went through many pages with a red pencil, making tiny marks.

When I got home, I gave a copy of BSR to my next-door neighbor. "Take a look," I said. "You might relax instead of killing someone."

"I have to protect myself," he said. "I am more man than you."

⁓

One day, a young woman came into the office to take the spelling test. I saw her through an open door. She was a small person, with sharp facial features. She looked older than I was but still relatively young. "I'd like to help you," I said, "but I can't."

"I like to read," she said, "especially about scientific things."

"Maybe we can meet and talk about it sometime."

"OK, maybe," she said.

"How about tomorrow?"

"I'm busy tomorrow, but you could call me in six months."

After she left, a woman I worked with said, "Well, I see you're not gay."

⁓

I received a letter addressed to Dr. Rutkowski, though I had no doctorate. The letter came from a researcher at a particle accelerator in Switzerland. The writer wanted to find peaceful applications for nuclear radiation. I wrote back, encouraging him to submit his article to the referees at GRG, and signed my letter "Dr. Rutkowski." How nice it would be, I thought, to be called Doctor all the time.

I didn't think my job as production editor of scientific journals would last long; I'd had enough of the entrails in AJDD. I had considered getting a doctorate and had even written to some schools to request applications. But when I saw the length of the required essays—on my interest in doctoral study and how I might fit into such a program—I decided it would be easier to go next door and get wasted with my Japanese neighbor. Sometimes he brought out his guitar and played a folk song. Other times, he waved his handgun around. I didn't know who would live and who would die, but I always left his place in time to go to bed and get up for work the next morning.

Coked Up

I WENT TO A FRIEND'S LOFT IN LOWER MANHATTAN FOR A party. The space was in a trendy neighborhood—my friend had financial means. She could afford a live in a loft, and her friends looked like they could live in lofts, too. I, on the other hand, was renting a small room in someone else's apartment.

Shortly, I saw a man spoon some white powder onto a mirror. He did the work on a coffee table, in front of several people. I was expecting the mirror to be passed from hand to hand, along with a straw or some other inhaler. But the man kept the glass plate for himself. Maybe he was looking at his face in it—he could have been a narcissist. The dust stayed on the mirror until he sniffed it.

I left without sampling the snow.

—

Over time, I became more cocaine savvy. I began to acquire small quantities of the drug for my own use. Once, I took a vial on a trip to visit a friend.

The friend met me with his car, and I took out my vial in the front seat. I had nothing to spread the powder on, so I used a piece of paper. I had no blade; I shaped the powder with a credit card.

"Do you want some?" I asked my friend.

"I'll try it," he said.

"How much do you want?" I asked.

"Just one."

"One line?" I said. "That won't be enough."

"That's all I'll take. No more."

After he'd inhaled, he said, "I don't feel anything. I don't see what's so special about this."

My friend started to drive and presently came to an intersection. He sped up to avoid an oncoming car. The vehicle turned out to be a police cruiser, and the cop at the wheel quickly pulled us over.

"I'm very sorry, officer," my friend said.

"You could have hit me," the man in uniform said.

"I was in a hurry."

"I could search this car," the cop said. "I could bring dogs and take everything apart. I could find what you have hidden. But I'll let you off with a warning—this time."

⁓

On another occasion, I got together with my off-and-on girlfriend, who was working as a temp on Wall Street. When she arrived at my room, she told me she hadn't slept. She'd spent the previous night inhaling cocaine with a stockbroker.

"His sister is a pop star," she explained.

When she told me the sister's name, I recognized it. I could even hear the sister's song, about a woman on the run, in my head.

"What about the coke?" I asked. "Is there any left?"

"I brought some for you," my girlfriend said.

She took out a rolled dollar bill. "Here it is," she said.

She unrolled the bill and scraped off the residue with a paring knife. There was enough for a couple of lines.

The flakes boosted my libido. When I approached my girlfriend, she said, "You're too excited. You need to back off."

I moved away, but only for a minute. I had to use my hands. I had to bring in my whole body. The next time I approached, she said, "You're scaring me."

I knew then that I would have to make a choice between using the drug or having sex. One or the other, but not both. Having both could be catastrophic. Who knew what I would do, while under the influence of the devil's dandruff?

—

I went to visit a friend who was in an art-rock band. I'd spent many hours standing in cramped spaces in burned-out buildings listening to his "music." He knew I was looking for coke.

Under his raised-platform bed, a baseball game was playing on a television set. "I like the green color," my friend said. "The field is beautiful."

The nail on one of his little fingers was about two inches long. He had painted the nail black.

"I don't have any cocaine," he said, "but I can give you this."

He handed me a small waxed-paper envelope with a cake-like substance in it. "It used to be powder," he explained.

He poked at the substance with his long fingernail. "Maybe you can break it up," he said.

"What is it?" I asked.

"Crystal meth."

He spooned out some of the gunk with his fingernail while I looked at the baseball field on the television. After sampling the crystal, I felt I could sit and watch TV for twenty hours straight. My heart was racing, and my breathing was fast and shallow—I was cranked up.

—

I went to a restaurant to meet my girlfriend. The place was small but crowded, and when I looked around I didn't see her. I waited a while, then tried to call her, but reached only her voice mail. After I'd waited a while longer, I left the place.

Later, I got a call from her.

"Where were you?" I asked. "I was looking for you."

"I was there," she said, "but I didn't see you."

"You were there?"

"I was sitting next to the wall with the mural. I ordered dinner."

I didn't recall seeing a mural in the restaurant. "Maybe we can meet another time," I said.

"Sure," she said, but I didn't pick up on the way she said it. A few days later, I realized I wouldn't hear from her again.

—

My job offered coverage for counseling, so I made an appointment with a therapist.

I inhaled a dose of coke before I went to see her. When I got to her "office"—a room in her house—we chatted. I answered her questions, then said, "I'm high on cocaine."

I expected her to be surprised, to say something like "Good gosh! You don't *look* like you're high on cocaine."

Instead, she asked, "Why are you telling me this?"

I wanted to say, "So you'll think I'm evil, like a devil." But I didn't say that. Instead, I said, "It makes it easier to watch baseball games. The ball field is beautiful."

"You sound disconnected," the therapist said. "Obviously, you don't know how to communicate. You'll have to see me twice a week."

—

My nose often bled at night. I wasn't aware of the bleeding while I was sleeping, but when I woke I saw where my blood had dripped and dried. My nostril linings were deteriorating. All of those particles had weakened my nasal membrane.

I could have switched to some other method of ingesting the drug. There were other parts of my body that were membranous and porous. But I didn't want to think about those parts. I didn't want to think about how to get powder through those orifices. The thought was too unpleasant.

I would just have to live without the drug, without a racing heart and pumping lungs. I would become dull and slow, like everyone else. The thought didn't sit well with me, but I tried to wrap my brain around it: I couldn't get coked up anymore; I had to stay out of the snow.

No Littering

INEVER LIKED CLEANING THE CAT LITTER, SO I JUST DIDN'T do it. I let the litter sit, in a corner of my place, and that arrangement was fine with my cat. He used the box whenever he pleased, and he didn't complain. But anytime someone visited me, that person would be hit with the fact that I hadn't cleaned the litter box. This person would usually be too polite to say, "This place stinks! Why don't you change the litter?" No, my guest would say something like "Do you enjoy having a cat?" I would know what that meant. It meant my guest was totally repelled by the days-old litter box.

I didn't know why I wasn't repelled. Maybe I was used to the sensation. Maybe it was one of those smells, like that of old wine, that I'd accepted. I actually liked the smell of fermented plant matter—the fumes and the yeast—but the cat trash went several degrees further. No one, myself included, really liked it. But I was floating on clouds of herbal smoke all of the years I had a cat, and my main purpose in life was to lose myself in more herbal clouds.

Most days, I'd come home to my empty place, and my cat would greet me at the door. He would rub against me, perhaps in a display of affection, but more likely to spread his scent onto my pants. We would build on that greeting by proceeding to the kitchen, where I would open a can of meaty food and place it on the floor, next to a bowl of water. I didn't pamper my cat: He ate from the can, and he had to use his teeth and claws to get the chunks out of the crevices. He drank water—with a backward lapping of his tongue. There was no milk for him.

And there was no fresh litter most of the time. I was too zoned out to provide it. I would chill in front of the television while my pet investigated the litter situation. He would never yowl over it. But sometimes he cleaned it himself by flinging dried lumps out of the bin and onto the floor. I would see those chunks later, and I would be reminded of what I should have done, but I wouldn't change the sand.

Not that I didn't like my cat. I did. We had a human/feline bond. I provided shelter and sustenance, and my cat provided company. He also provided protection from rodents. No mice lived with us—the mouser took care of them. Rats, however, were another story. These supersize rodents would sometimes come in from the street and hide. Once, I saw a healthy specimen, nose to the wall in a corner. The creature was trying to avoid detection by remaining perfectly still. I picked up my cat and brought him to look at the rat. I was expecting the predator to pounce and kill the intruder. But the cat didn't react; he just hung limply in my arms. When I put him down, he walked away. It was just me and the rat then. What I needed was an air rifle, but I had no weapons. I didn't believe in them. Well, I had a hammer and a broom, but I didn't have the gumption to use them. If I attacked with a hammer and a broom, I would just anger the rat, and I didn't want a large furious rodent trapped in my apartment. So I left the pest alone, and presently it ran from its corner, up a wall, and out an open window to the fire escape. From there, it must have dropped to the street, where it met its pack.

Perhaps my cat was sending me a message. If I'd been more attentive to his litter box, he might have been more helpful in expelling the invader.

As it was, I kept my distance, and my cat kept his. We didn't share a room. He had his space, and I had mine. I didn't want him sleeping on my bed; I didn't want his head on my pillow. The night of the rat's visit, however, I let my pet into my room. At some point in the night, he jumped onto my bed. And for whatever reason—whether I was acting out of deep, smoke-induced sleep or genuine compassion—I didn't push him away.

Cat's Teeth

WHEN I GOT HOME, I PUT MY KEY IN THE LOCK AND heard the sound of small paws running toward me. I opened the metal door and saw my orange-pinstriped cat. When he reached me, he rubbed his back against my leg. I walked into the kitchen area and put food on the floor. I didn't watch him eat, but I could hear him huffing over the container.

I heard a knock on my front door and opened it. My downstairs neighbor was there—she had her dog on a leash. The dog was a large energetic shepherd, and it wanted to come in. It reared up against its leash and beat at the air with its paws. It emitted loud panting sounds. My neighbor ruffled the fur on its neck, then put the dog in a headlock. "No!" she shouted. "No!"

I didn't know what my neighbor wanted. Whatever it was, it was probably trivial, something like a portion of sugar. But I didn't get to ask, because I'd forgotten about my cat. The sudden appearance of the dog alarmed him. The cat jumped onto my leg and latched on with his claws. He sank his teeth into my thigh and clamped down. His jaws were like the sides of a trap. He wouldn't, or couldn't, let go.

My neighbor dragged her dog away, and I kicked the cat off my leg. My pet didn't back off. He crouched as if he might spring again. I picked up a chair and held it in front of me, as if I were a lion tamer. I pointed the chair legs at the cat and thrust the piece of furniture forward. If I'd had a whip, I would have cracked it over my head. My cat looked like he'd gone wild. He'd gone back to the dawn of domestication.

The chair did the trick. The cat was cowed. He sank to the floor and eyed me. He looked like a tiny sphinx, ready to question me with a riddle, then kill me for the wrong answer. His outburst was over.

During the uproar, my neighbor and her dog had disappeared.

I looked at my injury and saw four small wounds where the cat's incisors had sunk in. The punctures indicated a wide jaw opening, a large hinge in a feline mouth. This cat could eat a squirrel, if not a horse.

I heard my phone ring. It was my downstairs neighbor. "Sorry about that," she said, "but you should have your cat tested for rabies."

At night, I was alone with my cat, who appeared harmless now, sleeping in a coil on the couch, nose under a hind leg, his side rising and falling gently with the intake and outflow of air.

When I went to bed, I heard him scratching at the outside of my shut door. Then I heard him howling. Usually, I ignored him, but on this night, again, I opened the door. He came in quietly. At some point during the night, he came up onto the bed.

Not a Pass

A WOMAN FRIEND AND I WERE SITTING ON A BENCH NEXT to each other, not touching. We were resting after wandering around an art museum separately—we'd planned to meet earlier but somehow didn't connect. We saw each other only as we were leaving.

I stretched my arm up, held it straight, then rocked it back.

"Was that a pass?" she asked.

I'd extended my arm to loosen my shoulder. My arm had been injured when I'd fallen. Moving the shoulder lessened the pain.

"No," I said, "it wasn't a pass."

On our bench, a pass could easily have been made. All I had to do was reach from my space into hers. Maybe I had that energy; maybe I was ready to go. But I wasn't sure where I would go. On the other hand, a pass might have been what she was expecting.

"I know a pass when I see one," she said.

I didn't recall making any forward move. I didn't recall making a rearward move, either. I had made no move, other than to loosen my shoulder.

"No," I said, "that's not what you saw."

From where we were sitting, we could watch an Alexander Calder mobile, made of sheet metal, wire, and paint. It was spinning so slowly that any change was barely perceptible. The piece reminded me of a mobile my father had made when I was a child.

"I saw you looking at me," she said.

I realized I was looking at her, so I averted my eyes, then brought them back to focus on her face. I couldn't tell if her expression was inviting or dismissive.

"I was making eye contact," I said.

I went back to watching the kinetic sculpture. My father sometimes took my family to cultural events at the state university, twenty miles from where we lived. He would have encouraged me to visit this museum.

"Don't try to hide it," she said.

I had nothing to hide. I slid my arm along the back of our bench. The gesture could have been interpreted as putting my arm around her, or as another exercise for my injury. "I'm just stretching," I said.

When I was an art student, I tried to make a mobile. I bent a wire hanger with pliers and glued biomorphic cardboard pieces to the struts, but I couldn't get the contraption to balance from a string.

"We can go now," she said.

She got up from the bench and walked away. I could have felt rejected, but I didn't. I did the polite thing, the chivalrous thing. I followed her through the museum exit. On the sidewalk, we parted on friendly terms.

"Let's do it again," I said.

A few weeks later, I heard she'd partnered with a guy I'd seen at a gathering of friends. He was tall, thin, and Caucasian, with light curly hair. He was the exact opposite of me.

To the Maxx

I HEARD A LOUD JINGLING, SO I GOT UP FROM MY CHILD-SIZE desk and picked up the landline. The device was connected to a wall jack with a long wire. I untangled the wire, carried the phone back to my desk, and sat at the child's chair. There wasn't enough room for my knees under the desktop, so I pushed my chair back. Still, I was stuck: The chair didn't swivel. I needed an office chair with casters, as well as an adult-size desk, but I wasn't about to upgrade. I'd brought the furniture from my parents' house and set it in my unfinished loft space. Why should I buy new things when I could have old things for free?

I spoke into the handset. "Hello," I said.

"Hi," a female voice said.

It was good to hear from my friend. Well, she was more than a friend, so it was more than good to hear from her. Because it was early evening, I thought we might have time to do something together. She might come to my place, or I might go to hers. If I went to her place, I might end up entertaining her children. I might have to read to them from kids' books while she made phone calls. She was addicted to talking on the phone, while I was not. I was addicted to other things.

If she came to my place, we might check out my child's bed, also brought from my parents' house.

She asked me to meet her at a store. The place had a suggestive name, beginning with two initials and ending with an intense descriptor: T.J. Maxx. I'd heard of the place—I expected that all of the items in it would be taken to the limit.

I had never been to a T.J. Maxx, but the store was fairly close by, in a fashionable neighborhood. I couldn't quite get there on foot, so I took the subway a couple of stops. I boarded the train in my dodgy neighborhood and got off where the streets were swept clean.

I went into the shop and found her in a carpeted area surrounded by mirrors. She was wearing a black leather dress that fit snugly, like a glove. She turned and gestured, holding her hands out from her waist. "Do you like it?" she asked.

"Yes, I do," I said.

I sat on a minimal seat—a smooth cube—and watched as she showed me some moves. She lifted her arms and flipped her hair as she spun around. I could see the dress from all angles, and I could smell the leather. The outfit cinched and lifted parts of her body. It was almost a harness. It matched her patent-leather shoes.

I wanted to join her in leather love. I wanted an outfit for myself: a jacket with loops and zippers, a vest and chaps, and stomper boots. All we needed to complete the ensemble was a motorcycle.

"Will you buy it for me?" she asked.

I understood then why I'd been called to the store. It had not been only to observe a modeling dance, a cat walk in a miniskirt, and a display of calfskin on human skin. It had also been to pay for something. I looked at the price of the dress and learned it was equivalent to a week's income. Still, I didn't think twice. I took out a plastic card and paid.

After the purchase, we went our separate ways: she back to her children, I to my loft decorated with child's furniture. I didn't know when I would next see her. Maybe it would be at a leather club, where wool clothing was not allowed. We would be dressed as brother and sister bikers. Who knew what we would do there, once we entered the garage?

At the Porn Review

I'D BEEN OUT OF WORK FOR A WHILE WHEN I WAS OFFERED a job at a men's magazine. I took the job—it paid better than unemployment compensation.

I was aware of the stigma. Women, and a good number of men, didn't like the magazine's view of women. According to some people, the publisher was a high-class pimp. One of my former colleagues said to me, "Congratulations on your new job at the *porn review*."

I'd heard the publication contained high-quality articles, interviews, and fiction. Many men bought it to read the text. They weren't ogling the photographs. The magazine had carried a two-part interview with a former Beatle and an investigative article on the overnight-delivery business. The photographs merely showed young women doing routine things—running on a beach or riding a horse—but without any clothes.

My task was to check statistics for ad-sales presentations. Prospective advertisers were to believe they would reach more men with ads in this magazine than they would through other publications. This magazine's readers bought massive amounts of cars, liquor, and cigarettes to get them through their free-spirited lives.

Part of my job was to write headlines for the sales pitches. One time, I was given a panel that showed a woman riding in a steeplechase. She was wearing breeches, tall boots, a helmet, and nothing else. Below the photo was a breakdown of costs per thousand ad impressions. For the chart headline, I wrote "More Jodhpur Dollar."

My supervisor liked the headline. "I get it," he said. "More jod per dollar! I'm sending this out with the sales reps."

Later, a sales representative said to me, "People think we're stupid, but we're not."

Another time, a model of the month came into the office. She must have had some role in sales promotion. I took note when she walked across the open doorway of my cubicle. She was wearing a business suit, not her birthday suit. But as soon as she left, I found the issue of the magazine that featured her. I matched the real-life person with the photos. I'd found the truth—of the model's self.

The magazine was connected to a nightclub in midtown Manhattan. I wasn't a member, but my work ID got me in. Once there, I expected to see flashing lights and hear disco music, all leading to a mysterious back room, but I didn't make it past the entranceway. I got stuck in a hallway, where women dressed like rabbits approached me. They were friendly but didn't ask if I wanted anything other than drinks. As well, I didn't ask for anything else. The club was a bar, and only a bar, with servers wearing floppy ears and cotton tails.

At home, I noticed that the women on a TV show I watched were dressed like the women in the club. The show took place aboard a spaceship that had no set course—it flew from planet to planet to find new civilizations. The female crew members wore short tight dresses and tall boots. The only things missing were the ears and the tail.

For one issue, the women in the company were invited to pose for photos. The feature was called "The Women of the Magazine." Participation was voluntary, but a number of women posed, either partially dressed or totally undressed. When the magazine came out, I recognized some of the women I worked with. They were people I saw every day, doing their jobs. I could have congratulated them—I should have congratulated them—but the whole idea seemed somehow off-kilter, skewed from the norm.

I wanted to make my living space into a bachelor pad. The wood floor was unfinished, and the kitchen had no cabinets. But there was a closet niche in the large living area. In it, I set up an entertainment booth. I put a stereo amplifier and turntable on shelves, and strung wires to speakers mounted near the ceiling. The amplifier generated a powerful wattage, and when I turned the volume up halfway, the empty space was filled with sound. I had a disco loft. I was ready to party. However, I later found that when the space was filled with people, the stereo could barely be heard.

After I'd worked at the magazine for a year, I was given a certificate of service. It was on thick, cream-colored paper suitable for framing. The paper was signed not by the publisher, who'd helped start a sexual revolution, but by his daughter, who was continuing his mission.

Outside the company, other media were taking the place of print. The car-driving, drinking, and smoking bachelors were watching cable television. In my office, people were leaving their jobs. I saw what was happening and started looking for another position. I found one at a business-trade magazine.

This magazine's readers also wanted the good life, but they found it through doing deals—buying low and selling high.

As I was leaving the men's magazine, one of my co-workers said to me, "You know, if you hadn't left voluntarily, you would have been fired."

That was OK with me. I had a least a week before my nose hit a new grindstone.

Hellfire

I MET A POLISH AUTHOR BY ACCIDENT IN A NIGHTCLUB. Before that, I had read books by the author, and, just before the encounter, I'd read a story by him in the soft-core porn magazine where I'd worked.

The author's magazine piece was an excerpt from his forthcoming novel. The story was set in an unnamed s/m club in New York's meatpacking district—an area filled with warehouses, weighing stations, loading docks, and idling trucks.

On this night, I was waiting in line with a woman friend to get into what looked like an abandoned building. The windows were boarded up, and the interior was dark. An iron railing marked where a cement stairway led from the sidewalk down to the basement. My friend was wearing a leather dress, and I had on my usual flannel and denim—what I thought of as Western. Several other kinksters were waiting patiently on the stairs. My friend recognized a man in line ahead of us. "That's the famous Polish author," she said.

He was a thin, tallish man, with curly hair and gnarly features, and he was wearing a camel-hair overcoat—an expensive and fashionable item. He looked as he would normally look; he wasn't wearing a disguise (as he was known to do);

he had no whiskers or beard. A dark-haired woman in business clothing stood with him.

We followed the cluster of people down the stairs. At the bottom was an electric light—a bare red bulb over the door, signaling the gate to the underworld. Upon entering, each guest had to sign a disclaimer stating that the club would not be responsible for any injury, embarrassment, or slander received inside.

The club was called Hellfire, and its decor was, if not hell-ish, depressingly diabolical. Along one brick wall was a plain, black bar. At the bar, some leather-clad sinners were drinking without remorse. Next to another wall was a small platform on which damnable acts could be staged. The centerpiece was a meat scale, complete with block and tackle. An evil entre-preneur was selling paddles, collars, cuffs, and gaff hooks at a folding table on the floor. The devil's dance mix came through speakers near the ceiling, with the sound turned up to distor-tion level.

Doorway-size holes that seemed to have been made with sledgehammers led off into darkness. Back there, in the inner-most pits, the eternal punishment would take place.

I stood with a drink, talked to my friend, and watched the author as he strolled around. I saw him greet people and chat with them. I didn't have much else to do. I had no whip to snap, paddle to swing, or lasso to throw. Whenever someone engaged in a Satanic ritual, a crowd would form, but my friend and I couldn't see through the packed bodies.

"I don't want to know what's happening," my friend said. "I can't watch."

At one point, I accosted the author as walked past. "Hi," I said. "My last name is similar to your last name."

"What's your last name?" he asked.

I told him and explained, "It rhymes with *house key*."

"I see," he said, and he told me his last name, which I'd known all along. "It almost rhymes with *on skis*," he added.

I introduced my friend, and he introduced his woman friend by her first name, Dora.

"Nice to meet you," we all said, but I doubted that all of us meant it.

I didn't tell the author which of his books I'd read or which of his experiences matched my own. I didn't admit that the atrocities he'd seen as a child in the Polish country-side reminded me of incidents I'd witnessed as a child in rural America. I didn't even tell him that I'd worked for a men's porn magazine that had just published an excerpt from his new novel.

"There's not much happening here," I said.

"You have to wait until about seven a.m.," he said, "for things to really get going."

I guessed he meant that the industrial scale in the middle of the floor would be put to use. Someone's weight would be measured there. The unfortunate one would then be put into a meat cooler and, when sufficiently chilled, would be loaded onto a truck idling outside. At that point, the real transport would begin.

"I don't know if we can wait that long," I said to the author.

He reached over and mussed my hair. "You're young," he said. "You can wait a long time."

At the Writers' House

MY ROOM IN THE WRITERS' HOUSE WAS ON THE TOP floor, in what had been the attic. I was at the house during a vacation from my job. The room had a slanted roof, and there was a window at one end. Through the window, I could see a church next door. Under one eave, I had a desk where I could do my work. Under the opposite eave was a walk-in closet, and someone had put a chair in there. I could sit on the chair and read in the closet. While sitting and reading, I might be visited by the Muse.

I liked my new room fine, but I wasn't used to it. On a previous visit, I'd been given a more standard room on the second floor. Now, however, I would get so caught up in my thoughts that I would automatically go to my former room, which was occupied by a young woman. One time, when I was returning from the shared bathroom, I turned her doorknob and walked in. She was in her bed, reading. She wanted to say something, but she was speechless. All she could do was make sounds like "Upp!" and "Nupp!"

An older woman gave me a ride to a grocery store in the nearby town. She called the favor a "mitzvah." At the store, named the Price Killer, I purchased a bottle of soy sauce. The bottle was relatively large, but there were no small bottles.

I brought the bottle back to our house and put it in the kitchen. A fellow resident found it and asked, "Who brought this? It will last for years!"

I decided to use the soy sauce liberally. I started by pouring it over chow mein I'd spooned from a can and heated on the stove. Later, I tried the soy on eggs and on tuna. I planned to use it at every meal.

—

I found a couple of bicycles stacked behind the house. When I inspected them, I discovered they had flat tires. I took the bike that had one flat instead of two and walked it to a service station. The station also sold hardware, so I bought a small item—a hook and latch—for later use.

The station had an air compressor in its parking area. I picked up the hose, applied the nozzle, and filled the flat. The tire felt hard, so I started riding. I covered a couple of hundred yards before I sensed a rhythmic thudding—a sign the tire was dead again. I walked the bike back to the house.

—

I brought the hook and latch to room of the woman I'd intruded on. I screwed the eyes into the door frame and panel. "Click the hook to keep the door shut," I suggested.

—

In the evening, I talked about my book with the people at the house. I had only one book, and it was small. It could fit in the palm of a hand. "I call it a novel," I said.

"What is it about?" the man who had commented on the soy sauce asked.

"It's fiction, based on my experiences."

"May I borrow it?"

I lent him the book, and he took it to his room.

⁓

Later, the woman who'd taken me to the store said to me, "Someone called you on the phone."

There was only one phone in the house, enclosed in a makeshift booth. Residents had to take turns using it, and during the day no one was likely to hear it ring.

"Who was it?" I asked.

"She wouldn't give her name, but she wanted me to come and get you."

"What did you say?"

"I said, 'We can't disturb people in their studios.'"

⁓

The call, I learned, was from my new girlfriend, who lived near me in the city. I wanted to invite her to visit. I would show her my room—and the walk-in closet, where someone had put a chair. One of us could sit in the chair and read, while the other sat at the desk under the eave. I wouldn't mind taking the chair. At other times, we could share my narrow mattress and look out the window at the church next door.

When I called her back, she asked, "Where were you?"

"In my room," I said.

"How many women are there at the house?"

"A few," I said. "Maybe six or seven,"

"That's too many! You must have been with one."

"You could come to visit," I said.

"It's over!"

⁓

The man who had borrowed my book returned it. I expected him to say something about the subject matter, to say that he found the content interesting, maybe even that he liked it. But all he said was, "Your book is not a novel; it's a novella. And it's not fiction; it's a memoir."

In the evening, the residents spotted a bat in the house. It was flying silently around the living room, echolocating to avoid obstacles. No one knew how to get rid of it. The bat's sudden changes in direction frightened some people; they thought the creature would land in their hair.

I found a fishing net and waited for the bat to fly past. Quickly, I swiped the bat into the mesh, walked outside, and shook it loose. It appeared to be stunned, but alive. With a cloth-covered hand, I lifted it to the outside wall of the house. It stayed there, motionless.

When I came back in, a man asked me, "Did you kill it?"

"I think it will drop off the wall and fly," I said.

At night, half asleep, I automatically tried to go into my former room. I wasn't thinking about the new occupant, the young woman who might be reading in her bed. I came out of the bathroom, stumbled to the door, and turned the knob. But she had latched the hook I'd installed, and the door wouldn't open more than a crack. The room was dark inside. I called, "Sorry!" through the crack, shut the door, and walked carefully upstairs to my attic room.

Meeting the Train

O N ANOTHER OCCASION, I WENT TO A LARGER ART COLONY. There, a freight train would stop under a bridge every evening. The track ran between farm fields and patches of trees before it came to the overpass. My colleagues, some of whom had arrived before me, knew when the train would stop, and they looked forward to its arrival.

"Let's meet the train this evening," someone would say.

"Yes, it comes after dinner," someone else would say.

There wasn't much to do for entertainment at the retreat. We could walk one way on a back road between the fields, or we could walk the other way on the same road.

Usually, only women would go to the bridge. I didn't mind not going. I didn't know most of my companions, anyway. We were doing our work together only for a short time.

I knew one woman, however, from years before, when we'd been at the same college. I hadn't seen her since, and I was eager to talk to her.

"Why don't we take a walk after dinner," I asked her, "just you and me, so we can catch up?"

"We can do that," she said, "but not now. Sometime before you leave."

It seemed she didn't trust me enough to go for a walk with me. Maybe she thought I would do something crazy. I might get too excited, say or do something I shouldn't.

One afternoon, I walked by myself to the bridge. I looked at the rails—laid straight and firm on a gravel lane. On either side of the track, trees formed a tunnel. Leafy vines smothered their trunks and branches. Around me, cicadas whined like invaders from space. But no train came.

Again at dinner, my new friends wanted to meet the train. "We went yesterday," one woman said.

"It was fun," said another.

"You should go," they said to me.

But I didn't go. Instead, I stayed in my room. I wanted to be away from the other residents.

As I lay there, I began to sense the train's presence. I heard a long, low note that could have been an ambulance arriving to cart someone away, or a helicopter hovering to save a life. Then I realized it was the train's horn blowing. The freight carrier was rolling close to my studio, as it did every evening—I just hadn't noticed it.

⁓

Shortly before I left the house to return to my home, I joined my colleagues on a "train run." The woman I'd known at school also came along. Apparently, having other people around made her feel comfortable with me. As we walked, I asked about her life.

She said that after she'd received her graduate degree, she'd been offered three full-time teaching jobs. She chose the one farthest from where she lived. Eventually, she received tenure there.

"You had good luck with your applications," I said.

"You can't apply for a teaching job," she said. "You have to be asked. If you're not asked, don't bother to apply."

As we approached the bridge, I didn't believe the train would actually stop, but it was waiting when we arrived. The locomotive was parked below the cement railing.

The women waved to the men in the lead car. The men leaned out of their windows and waved back. Then the drivers got out and stood on a metal step of the locomotive. They were wearing the gray uniform of the railroad company.

"Hello!" they called.

"Hello!" the people with me called back.

After a short while, the trainmen got back into their cabin. The whistle blew, and a line of freight cars moved under us.

After the spotting, my former schoolmate gave a demonstration of her art. She stood in a corner, facing outward, and held a black marker behind her head. She moved the marker back and forth, drawing a zigzag line on the white walls. As she drew, she slowly slid toward the floor. Her reach became shorter as her body moved away from the wall. Her finished drawing looked like a small tornado cloud.

That night, I lay awake, thinking I might hear a train. At two or three in the morning, one came. I heard a long note from the horn, then the noise of wheels on rails. I thought it would be exciting to hop a ride. I didn't know where we would go, but we could go anywhere the tracks led.

The sound of metal on metal lasted a long time.

Chainsaw

ON MY WAY HOME FROM MY JOB, I STOPPED AT A below-street-level restaurant called Jade Mountain. Inside, there was no sign of a mountain, but murals of green-leafed plants decorated the dimly lit walls. I picked up my take-out order and climbed the steps to the sidewalk.

In my spartan living space, I rolled my office-style chair over to a low table in front of my television and bent over the food. I put on a tape of a movie that was so popular I'd heard teenage boys call out its title, *Chainsaw*, while I sat in a theater waiting for a different movie. I sat and ate my brown-sauce dish while I watched the screen.

Outside my window, a fire truck screamed past. Its siren drowned out the voices on the TV, but only for a minute.

When I finished eating, I cleared off the table and continued watching. The film followed a group of teenagers as they drove to an old homestead in a remote part of Texas. The youngsters ended up at a strange house—actually, a slaughterhouse—where one by one they were killed. The exception was a young woman who was only tortured. She escaped by jumping out a window. The violence was almost abstract; it looked like ballet. When a buzzing came over the soundtrack,

I knew a motorized saw was running somewhere. Whenever the killer appeared, he waved the murder weapon like a feathered fan over his head.

—

At my office, I brought an idea to my supervisor. My pitch was contained in one sentence on a piece of paper. I stood at one wing of the boss's desk and made my case. "I'd like to report on licensing in movies," I said. "Licensing is big business."

"What kind of licensing?" the editor asked.

"The licensing of music, like music for a movie in Texas."

"Who would want to license that?"

"Lots of producers make movies in Texas."

"Do you have any producers who will talk to you about licensing?"

"Not yet."

"Do you know of any sound editors who will give a comment?"

"No."

"How about recording-studio directors?"

"I contacted one, but her publicist said she wouldn't participate."

The boss's face became red. He slid his chair back from his desk and jumped up. "You can't do this!" he shouted.

The people around us didn't say anything.

I went back to my workstation and started to edit an article by a writer whose text was dirty. Where she didn't have a fact, she inserted a TK. She added a TK to almost every one of her sentences. In fact, her nickname in the office was "TK."

I didn't complain about TK's writing. Sooner or later, the blanks would be filled in. I just hoped her stories wouldn't be published with the TKs still on the page.

On my way to the restroom, I saw the boss in the hallway. He was standing next to a woman—our magazine's star columnist. He was touching her face with his hand. She had her back to the wall.

"I've been watching you," I heard him say. "You're so young."

She stood there while the man fingered her hair. I walked past them and pretended not to notice. When I came back, they were gone.

—

I prepared my living space for a party. I'd gotten rid of the child-size furniture I'd brought from my parents' house, but I hadn't replaced it. I took my bed—a mattress kept rolled during the day with rope—out of the main room and propped it on a public-stairway landing. I cleared off the door plank I used for a desk and put drinks and snacks on it.

When my co-workers arrived, a man asked where I slept.

"My bed is in the hallway," I said.

"Do you always sleep in the hallway?"

"No, it's wrapped up."

"His bed is in the hallway," the man explained to the other guests.

During the festivities, a couple of people got drunk.

The woman called TK stood in my closet-size kitchen and started yelling. She leaned forward from her waist and put her hands on her knees. I couldn't tell exactly what she was saying, but I heard her referring to me and my people. "You should go back to your people," she was saying.

A young man came up to her and asked, "Haven't we met before?"

"No," she said.

"Come on," he said. "We must have met somewhere. I know we did. Where was it?"

He reached toward her, but she batted his hand away. "We haven't met," she said.

At a late hour, most of my guests had left, but the young man was still harrassing TK. He was also drunk, and she was ignoring him. He turned to me and got choked up. "She doesn't like me," he said, sobbing.

The party ended when another young man played a video of a spoken-word performance he'd given. The performance was so loud and incoherent it cleared almost everyone out of my apartment.

The only partiers left were TK and me. "

"Maybe you could come visit again," I said. "I just watched this movie where everyone was running around, yelling, 'Chainsaw!'"

"Nothing like a little violence," she said.

Lines and Maps

IN THE MORNING, MY MOTHER GAVE ME A RIDE TO A SUBWAY station so I could catch a train to work. I was glad she was with me, because she hardly ever came to the city. She usually didn't have the energy to make the trip, and driving in traffic frightened her. We sat in her car until it was time for me to go down the stairs to the platform.

My father wasn't around. I hadn't seen him in years. Oddly, I thought he was doing something, somewhere. Maybe he was also going to work. Then I remembered he wasn't around at all. That is, on this earth.

After she dropped me off, my mother would drive back to her home. I knew she would speed on her way there. I didn't see how she would avoid getting caught and fined. But if she was stopped, she would say, "I'm not from here! I'm Chinese!" and the police would leave her alone.

Before I went to my workplace, I talked to a young man about a new job. I wanted to switch to a better employer. This man had a beard, and he talked quickly. I didn't understand what he did for work—it was beyond what I did—but I said I wanted the job. I could handle it. After all, I was working.

"Where are you working?" he asked.

"At a weekly trade magazine," I said.

The weekly production process didn't mesh with the new technology my interviewer used.

The man said, "I know someone you used to work with. Do you know her?"

I remembered an efficient woman with wavy hair who sat a few desks away from me. We hadn't interacted much. "Yes," I lied, "I totally know her. I remember her well."

⌒

I was excited about the possibility of new job, so I rode my bike to the neighborhood around the prospective office. I rolled down one street and planned to follow a parallel street back. But when I turned and traveled one block, the parallel street wasn't there. I'd taken a curved street, not the straight one I wanted to be on.

I passed a palm reader's storefront, marked with a mystical hand illustration. Thinking I could get directions, I stopped. Inside, I said to a young woman, "I'm looking for a certain street. Do you know where it is?"

The young woman was wearing a long skirt and bangles. She could have been a hippie or a Romani. I didn't think she was a Romani.

"No," she said. "But I can give you a reading."

I showed her my dominant right palm, and she looked at one of the creases—it started close to my first finger and curved down below my middle finger.

"Your 'head' line is separated from your 'life' line," she said. "That means you seek adventure. But it is bent, not straight, so you have unrealistic expectations.

"How so?"

"The good news is, you'll get married and have a child. The bad news is, you'll be doing your workday job for a long time."

"Who will I marry?" I asked.

"Someone new."

I wanted to ask, "Do you have a street map?" but knew she couldn't provide one.

I started to ride back the way I came, and when I stopped at an intersection, a younger rider stopped next to me. "You go ahead," I said. "I'm slow."

"I know," he said.

My backpack was heavy, as heavy as a baby carrier. But a baby carrier would have a waist belt and side supports in addition to shoulder straps, and it would not zip closed. My backpack was unoccupied.

—

I wanted to visit my mother, but I had no car, so I reserved one through a rental service. There was no direct bus or train to where she lived. The bus trip took twelve hours, and the nearest train station was forty miles from her house.

I called to tell her I would visit, but she told me not to come. "Your brother is here," she said. "You wouldn't be happy."

"Why not?" I asked. "I thought I was always welcome."

"He's not feeling well. He doesn't want to see you."

"I already made a plan."

"It's easy to cancel it."

I had been looking forward to seeing my mother, but I didn't want to upset my brother. More importantly, I didn't want him to upset me—even his silence and disinterest would bother me—so I canceled my trip.

I walked until I came to the East River, then followed a paved path downtown. The water was flowing backward because the river was actually an estuary; the water's direction changed with the tides.

I looked over my shoulder and saw a storm coming over the tops of skyscrapers. The buildings were massive, but the clouds dwarfed them. Once over the buildings, the storm would cover the tree-filled park where I was walking. This storm would carry great force. I looked for an anvil-shaped cloud—the beginning of a tornado—but didn't see one.

I thought I could get home before the storm hit, so I picked up my pace. The air was calm, then a strong wind blew and rain started to fall. I was still a few blocks from where I was going. I heard the crackle of lightning—it seemed to strike beside me, close enough for the current to travel through the ground and set my shoes smoking—and a report of thunder immediately after the flash. I looked down; my shoes were unscathed.

I saw that I had arrived at the palm reader's shop again and went inside. I told the young Romani—if she was a Romani—that I'd like another reading.

"Let's look at your 'fate' line," she said, and I showed her my right palm.

"The line starts at the base of your thumb. You have a strong attachment to family and friends. But the line isn't straight. It's jagged. External factors will change your life."

"Can I change my destiny?" I asked.

"You're lucky you have a fate line. Some people don't even have one."

⌒

I chose a book from the many I owned, opened it, and saw a map of part of the city: the park next the river, where I'd just been. I had heard this area would be torn up soon. The trees would be cut down to make way for a flood-control project. I turned the pages and saw various neighborhoods, farther and farther from where I lived. I flipped the pages backward and returned to where I'd started.

I wanted someone to accompany me on my next trip. I went outside and came to a small open area. I looked around and decided to ask a man I didn't know. This man was asleep, sitting in a lawn chair with his head on a metal table. He was elderly; he had white hair. He looked like my father on a long-past binge. This man was going to make this journey himself soon. I was tired, too, but not as tired as he was. I was not going to sleep with my head on a table.

Treatment

I WAS VERY TIRED WHEN I ARRIVED AT MY MOTHER'S HOUSE. My brother had been living there for a while, after he'd been diagnosed with cancer. Usually, my mother took him for treatment, but I wanted to take him during this visit. Following his instructions, I arrived at six-thirty in the morning.

"You'll drive," he said.

"OK," I said. "You'll tell me where to go."

I drove for about an hour, past farms and small towns in the Pennsylvania Wilds, to a medical center in a somewhat larger small town.

My brother checked in at the clinic, and we waited for what seemed a long time—more than an hour—in an outer room. No one else was waiting. Apparently, my brother wanted to be first. "When they put in the needle," he said, "I'll sing a song."

He dropped to the floor in the waiting room, on his hands and toes, and did some push-ups. "I usually run in the morning," he said, "in the dark."

"Be careful," I said. The roads where he lived were narrow and had no walkways.

There were a few other people in the chemo room. Maybe they were residents of the hospital. They seemed to be in good spirits, sitting in reclining chairs, with IV bags attached to wheeled poles next to them. When the nurses hooked him up, my brother sang a line of a song about the Southland. He sat for a while, chatting with a couple of the other people.

"No one says why they're here," he said to me. "No one says exactly what they have."

After a few minutes, he said, "We can walk around. We'll roll everything with us."

Pulling his medication pole, he led me through the corridors to a small room with couches. As we sat there, a minister came by. He wanted to talk about spiritual things, but my brother wanted to talk about local sports.

"You know," my brother said, "I still hold a high-school record for the triple jump."

"That's great," the minister said.

"I made the fifth-longest jump in school history."

"Have you made any preparations?"

"For what?"

"For your family, your friends."

"I want my ashes to go into a Pacific bay, and I want my money to go to the aquarium on the bay."

The treatment took half a day. When we left the clinic, I was more tired than I was in the morning. I asked my brother if he could share the driving, but he said he couldn't. I fought to keep my eyes open and on the road at all times.

"I had my choice of jobs in California," he told me. "I had interviews with good firms, and they made big offers. All I had to do was choose the best one. I worked there for years. If I got a job there now, I'd go back tomorrow. I hate it here."

"I hope you can go back," I said. I wondered how much time he would have, if he returned, but I didn't say anything.

"Here, everyone thinks I'm a loser. You think so; our mother thinks so. The only people who don't think so are the people at the gym."

"*I* don't think so," I said.

⁓

When we returned to my mother's house, I talked to my sister on the phone. She was living in California, where she'd gone to school years earlier. "He still runs in the morning," I said, "when it's dark."

"He told me that if he gets hit by a car, he won't mind," she said.

"He asked us to scatter his ashes off the California coast."

"He told me we could flush them down the toilet."

"I'll come out there," I said.

"OK. We'll meet at the shore."

I went to the front of my mother's house and sat on the concrete steps leading down from the front door. In front of me was a cornfield, a diary farm, and the hill called Rattlesnake Mountain. Soon, my brother came out and sat next to me. He put an arm around me. The arm was strong and firm, in spite of the debilitating treatments.

"Do you think I'll see our grandmother when I get to the other side?" he asked.

"I don't know. Maybe. I really don't know."

Class Walk

I WAS ON MY WAY TO A CLASS I WAS SCHEDULED TO TEACH, but the class hadn't started and the room was in a new location. I had the street address, but I hadn't been to the building before.

I left on time and thought I had enough time to get to where I needed to be, but I was running late. My brother was with me, though I didn't know why he was there. I hadn't seen him in a while.

We walked uptown, heading for a certain city street, but it was slow going. Snow covered the streets and sidewalks, and our feet slid with every step.

"It's time to run," I said, and started to jog. I was surprised I could run at all.

My brother easily kept up with me. He was in good shape. "You know," he said, "when I got out of treatment, I couldn't run a hundred yards. Now, I can go for miles."

The class, even though it was happening only once, was being observed by a faculty member, and I didn't know what would happen if I wasn't on time. I didn't know if I'd be able to make my presentation during the second part of the lecture. It was a three-hour class, but I might be more than an hour late.

Would the observer wait that long? Or would he or she leave and reschedule for a time when I wouldn't be there?

My brother and I were walking fast now—the jogging was over—on streets that were unfamiliar to me. We had started going uptown on a major avenue, but somehow we had left it. I could see the avenue to our right, with cars and buses moving on it.

It didn't occur to me to take a bus or a cab.

"What's the plan?" I asked my brother.

"We'll play it by ear," he said.

When we arrived at the corner where the college was supposed to be, none of the buildings were recognizable. I saw a large brick structure, low and about a block long, that resembled a factory, but a sign over the door said it was a cooking school. Maybe the campus of my school would be next to it.

I looked around to find the time of day and saw a large clockface on a tower. The hands of the clock told me the start time of my class had passed.

My brother turned to leave. He was going to his home, far from where I lived. However, he gave me his phone number. "Don't write to me," he said. "Don't take twenty minutes or half an hour to write a letter. Just call me and talk for five minutes."

When I arrived at the classroom, I saw it was divided into two sections. I took my position in one section and started to speak. I didn't know if the students in the other part of the room could hear me. Probably they could. But they certainly couldn't see me or the notes I put on the whiteboard.

I wanted the students to hand in a short essay, but I realized I hadn't assigned the reading they needed for preparation. No one had done the essay. So we started a language exercise. I wrote random words on the board—"dig," "digital"—but I didn't know if the students would be able to use these words in sentences. That might be asking them to do too much, to write sentences that contained random words yet followed a logical sequence. Nevertheless, that was their assignment. I sat at the front desk while they did their work. I scanned the attendance sheet and wondered what had happened to the students who weren't there. I imagined that close relatives of theirs had died and the students had been called to attend the funerals.

After the class, I walked out to the street and spotted a stand of bicycles for rent. I uncoupled a bike from the rack and rode downtown. But as I looked at the street numbers, I saw they were rising. I saw 112th Street, then 116th Street. I reversed direction, but the same thing happened: The street numbers ascended. I left the grid entirely and found myself on a two-lane road—a blacktop with a double line down the middle and single lines along the edges. I was in a no-passing zone; I could see that. But otherwise, I didn't know where I was. I didn't know why I was on a road passing through fields. This section looked like the area where my brother lived. I couldn't understand why this barren countryside was attached to the island, filled with buildings, where I lived.

After the Passing

IN THE EARLY MORNING, I LOOKED OUT MY HOTEL WINDOW and saw only whiteness—a cloud over the valley. In the fog, everything was a ghost of itself. The buildings (a garage, a hotel next door) were faint replicas of structures. A fast-food restaurant was a vague box with a yellow "M" floating over it.

On the road, the vehicles were ghost conveyances, piloted by phantom drivers. Logos on the sides of trucks weren't clear. Was that rig really an ice cream truck? I made out two huge ice cream cones painted on the side of the trailer. But maybe the images weren't ice cream cones. My eyes could have been playing tricks on me.

Traffic lights glowed like blurred disks over the highway. The vehicles around me appeared as headlights and taillights, with no shapes between.

After I'd covered a couple of miles in my rented car, I saw more light in the sky. Gradually, the fog lifted and the highway became clear. The sun shone from a blue sky onto lush green trees. Along the sides of the road, orange clouds clung to the hills.

~

I'd been called home because my brother had died. I was apprehensive about what I'd find, not because I expected to find anything in particular, but because the situation was strange. My brother used to live there; now he didn't. Maybe his spirit would occupy the empty space. Maybe the spirits of other departed relatives would be there with him. I prepared myself for a convention of souls.

⌒

When I got to my mother's house, she told me the story of the passing. I watched and listened as she described my brother's last attack. She acted out her part, using as props medical paraphernalia—an IV drip stand, rubber tubes, a vacuum machine.

"I couldn't clear his lungs," she said. "I couldn't help him breathe."

"You did all you could," I said. "No one could have done more."

"If I'd learned better, I could have saved him."

"No one could. That's what the EMTs said."

She heard me but didn't respond.

⌒

I went to a hardware store to borrow a bolt cutter. The first person I asked didn't want to lend the tool. But the manager seemed to know me.

"We went to high school together," he said.

"I remember your brother and sister," I said.

"Your brother would come in here to make copies," he continued.

"Oh, you knew him."

"I knew he was sick. What was it? Cancer?"

"Yes."

"You know what I like to do?" he said. "Sail on the lake— you know the place. I have a small boat. You should try it. If you go out at night, you'll be the only one there."

⌒

I brought the bolt cutter to my mother's house and severed a chain wrapped around two bicycles. A hand-lettered sign on the bikes said they belonged to my brother.

"You can ride when you visit," he had said to me, but he was hardly ever there when I visited, and he never unlocked the bikes.

My mother saved the chain and padlock from the bikes. "I don't want to do anything he wouldn't want me to do," she said. "These are his; they're part of him."

⌒

I remembered my brother had held odd jobs. He'd told me he'd sold his blood, washed cars, and worked as a doorman at a strip club. But he also had a license to practice law. He didn't make much money from that, he'd said.

"Most of my clients are in prison," he'd explained.

"What about your clients who aren't incarcerated?" I'd asked.

"They pay me with bags of potatoes."

My mother and I looked around my brother's bedroom and found many thousands of dollars in cash. The twenties were on his dresser, and the hundreds were in bank envelopes on his desk. "I gave him a twenty every morning," my mother said. "I told him to buy something for himself."

In addition to receiving my mother's donations, he was getting paid, and his expenses were low because he was living with my mother. He paid for gas, the occasional vehicle repair, and law books.

"You should put the cash in a bank," I said to my mother. "You shouldn't leave it lying around."

My brother hadn't written a will.

As I sat at his desk and scanned the room, I saw piles of unworn clothes, many opened and unopened personal-care items, several broken computers, and a couple of dead television sets. There was a cleared area between clothes and papers on his bed where he could sleep.

I discovered that he had large accounts at various banks. Apparently, he had been making lots of money, presumably from legal work. Either that, or he had saved cash from his younger days, when he'd had good jobs.

I gathered cans of hairspray, bottles of deodorant, containers of bronzer, and bars of soap and stuffed them into a plastic garbage bag. I carried the heavy sack out of the house and set it where it could be picked up and carted away.

Later, I saw that my mother had retrieved the bag.

"Some of this is still good," she said.

I looked to see if any of the items were unopened. All had been used. I replaced the garbage bag in its pickup spot.

I called a lawyer friend of my brother's, who expressed his condolences.

"He was good at getting arbitrations, settling disputes in court," the friend said. "I would have liked to get more of those myself."

"Did they pay well?"

"Not really, but they were hard to get."

"Did he owe you money?" I asked. "Did you owe him?"

"No, but he gave me some silk-screen prints made by your father. Do you want them back."

"No," I said. "You can keep them."

My mother lit an incense stick and placed it on the floor under a framed photo. The photo showed the grave markers of her parents, whose ashes were stored in a cemetery plot in China. There wasn't enough space for full-size graves.

"Thank you, Mama," my mother said as she made a praying shape with her hands. "Thank you, Papa."

She thanked my brother, too.

"What kind of incense is that?" I asked.

She looked at the package and said, "It's called Silver Moon."

I drove to a nearby lake in the evening and parked in the empty asphalt area. The night was warm—it was pleasing to be outside.

At the waterline, I found a small boat pulled up onto the sand. It looked like a rowboat, and it held one paddle. The boat wasn't secured.

I pushed the boat onto the water and jumped in as it slid from shore.

In the middle of the lake, I couldn't see trees or other surroundings. The sky provided no light. There were no other boats on the water, and there was no sound.

I stayed out for a long while, drifting around. To change direction, I leaned forward and dug in with the paddle.

Later, the sky brightened and a half-moon rose.

I stared at the half-moon for a few seconds—not too long, because I'd seen it countless times before. If this were the first time I'd ever seen it, I didn't know what I'd think. I wouldn't understand why this object was in the sky. I wouldn't understand why it had dark and light patches, how its phases worked, or how it moved around its axis and around the earth. I would have been like a primitive human or a lesser primate, staring at a new celestial body. I might have thought the object would appear only once. I wouldn't have believed it would reappear at regular intervals until the end of time, as I understood time.

part three

Strangers in the Night

I MET A STRANGER—OR A STRANGER MET ME—AT A BLIND professor's house. A party was happening there; I'd heard about it while I was at a café across the street. Someone told me there was a gathering, so I went.

The professor was sitting on his couch and smoking, dropping ashes near a tray on a cushion. He was shaking hands with anyone who approached. "Introduce yourself," he was saying. "I'm blind."

I told him my name, and he said, "I haven't seen you for a hundred years."

I made my way to the back "porch," which was actually a fire-escape landing. When I looked over the railing, I could see people schmoozing below. From the apartments around the courtyard, neighbors occasionally yelled at the partiers to shut up.

At one point, a young woman on the fire escape called my name, and I went toward her. She told me we worked together, in the same building but on different floors. "I saw you at the laser printer," she said. "You were wearing a button-down shirt and a tie."

I didn't remember seeing her there, but we must have shared the elevator or passed each other in the building's "lobby," which was more like a hallway. We might have walked next to one another in the column of drones heading to and from work.

"That was my dork suit," I said.

Her neck-length hair went out to one side in a wave. Her face, visible in the half-light, drew my attention. We seemed to have chemistry, though I didn't know what that meant; I was no chemist. We seemed to be simpatico, but I knew even less about that. It was enough that she knew my name and had called out to me. That sort of acknowledgment had not happened often. In fact, it had not happened before. True, some people called to me without knowing my name—they called me Hombre or Mister or You—while others knew my name but chose not to address me at all.

I left the party but soon had second thoughts. Where was I going? Home? What was there for me? A movie on TV, a magazine on the floor?

I went back to the party—that was the key move, that I went back—and the person who'd called to me was still there, on the metal porch over the dark garden. She was almost hidden by people's heads and shoulders.

"I came back," I said.

"Why?"

"To see you."

⁓

Later, the blind professor liked to tell anyone who would listen that we'd met at his party. "They met on the back landing," he would say. "Right there, on the fire escape. He wasn't even invited. He just showed up."

Island Visit

WHEN MY NEW WIFE AND I ARRIVED ON A GREEK ISLAND in late winter, we saw a row of sales counters for U.S. car rental agencies in the air terminal, but we had made no arrangements with them. We found our local rental desk at the end of the line.

When we received our car, we saw a large decal in the back window that said TOUR RENT. Anyone who didn't know why we were here would know why now, when they read the sign.

We soon learned that our car had a bad tire—one with a slow leak. Every time we filled up with gas, we needed to fill up with air.

The car had a standard transmission. I was the only one who could drive it, though "drive" was an overstatement. While stopped on hills, facing upward, the car stalled. When the engine cut out, I had to put the transmission in neutral, step on the brake, turn the key, step on the clutch, shift into first, and move my foot quickly from the brake to the gas. I gunned the engine while releasing the clutch—slowly.

The roads were frequently blocked by sheep. We had to wait until they crossed before we could proceed. Stretches of pavement were one lane, so progress was slow. Anytime I had to wait for an approaching car to pass, our car might have stalled.

A joke about shepherds and sheep came to mind. A shepherd desired a sheep, but the problem was keeping the sheep close enough to couple with it. Sheep were skittish, and they could run fast. So the shepherd had to put the hind legs of the sheep into the front of his rubber boots. That way, the sheep couldn't escape.

I didn't repeat this joke aloud.

We were on a road that narrowed, but we kept following it. The road didn't look right. It was straight, not winding as we'd expected. It led through a double row of decorative trees. We were funneled into a town we had wanted to bypass. All of the streets in the town had only one lane. We turned around and went back along the road between the perfect trees.

~

We made it up a mountain road and came to a town called Spili. We stopped beside a fountain. The motion of the water made me think about the name Spili, as if this was the town of "spilling water." Someone could bottle this water and sell it, even though it was free in the first place. The brand name could be Spili Spring, or Spiliani.

Wasn't that what beverage companies did, drew water from a spring? Or did they just take tap water and give it a fancy name, like that of a South Pacific island, and put it in nicely designed bottles on supermarket shelves?

We filled our plain bottles with Spili water before we traveled down the mountain. I later learned that *spili* meant *cave*.

~

We looked for a hotel on the coast of the island, but we didn't see a place that was open. We went into a café—we had nowhere else to go—and asked where we might stay. A woman picked up a phone and made a couple of calls, explaining that a visiting couple was looking for a room.

In time, a man appeared and told us we could stay in his hotel. He would open it for us.

There were no other guests in the hotel, and there was no heat. The night was chilly. But we were grateful for the room—it cost next to nothing, and we had each other's company. During the night, I reached over to my partner, but she was asleep. In the morning, she asked, "Did you try to hug me last night?"

"Yes," I said.

"Well, I'll hug you back now."

~

During the day, we walked on a pebbled beach and decided to take photos. For each shot, we had to make sure the film was advanced—we didn't want a double exposure. We needed to focus manually by twisting the ring around the lens. We had to adjust the f-stops so that the image would be bright enough. Then we released the shutter and hoped for the best—we wouldn't be able to see the photos until the film was developed.

We took turns standing on the beach in our jackets—the month was February—while we snapped each other's picture. We saw no one else for a half mile in either direction.

North Africa lay across the water. "It might be warmer there," my new wife said.

"Yes," I said, but I didn't know if the climate was really better across the water.

We went to a restaurant that didn't seem to be open for business. But the front door wasn't locked, and people were inside, so we walked in and sat at a table. It was a dreamy kind of place, with a painting of a ship on the sea and the moon in the sky.

There was a bucket filled with water on the floor, and in the bucket was a live fish. We understood we could have that fish for dinner, but we decided against it. We didn't want the sacrifice on our hands.

After dinner, we ordered shots of a clear liqueur called *raki*, and we were given more portions for free.

I had a laughing attack. "This drink is Turkish," I said. "It's not even Greek."

"Don't drink too much," my wife said.

"We're near the cave where Zeus was born," I said. "Were his parents drinking *raki* when he was conceived?"

I amused myself to such a degree that I fell off my chair and rolled on the floor. "I've drunk myself under the table," I announced.

My wife stayed in her seat. "Please get up," she said.

The restaurant's proprietor wasn't upset. She seemed to expect this kind of behavior from foreigners. She gave us another round of drinks.

Wife was a word that wasn't easy to get used to. I preferred *spouse*; it was easier for me to say. Was there any difference between the two? *Spouse* was more abstract, more archaic, than *wife*. *Teammate* was even better. I had someone on my team, someone who would watch my back, run interference against opponents, charge with me toward the goal. That was the kind of person I wanted with me, as I tried to advance against bigger, meaner players, people who would enjoy nothing more than to bulldoze their way over me.

But *teammate* didn't say enough when checking into a hotel.

Did the "teammate" want her own room? The staff couldn't tell from that description. If I meant *wife*, I should have said it. "I'm here with my wife," I should have said.

And she would have said, "I'm here with my husband."

That sounded right.

Bus Rides

I SAW TWO MEN SITTING NEAR ME ON THE BUS. THEY WERE crowded next to each other on the back seat, over the engine. One man was smaller, the other larger. I heard the larger man say to his accidental neighbor, "You have to move."

The smaller man did not move, perhaps because he didn't understand.

"*Maricón*," the larger man said. "Do you know what that means?"

The larger man started to shove the smaller one, bumping him with his elbow and hip.

The smaller man made no reply, but his face became red with rage.

"You are a *maricón*," the larger man repeated.

The larger man was carrying a bag with something inside it, something delicate made of wood and glass. Pieces of a frame stuck out of the bag. Maybe the object was a work of art.

When the larger man got off the bus, the smaller one followed. He grabbed the bag out of the man's arms and threw it to the ground. He stomped on it, shattering the object inside. Then he ran away, along the sidewalk. The larger man looked shocked and angry, but he didn't chase the smaller one. Maybe he knew he was not fast enough to catch him.

I got off the bus and walked to the office where I worked. My assignment was to check facts, and I proceeded to do that. I believed the facts I was checking were correct, but I wasn't sure they were. In any case, I didn't want to check them again. I was on a time clock and wanted to be done.

It was Friday, and I told my fellow worker that I wouldn't be back on Monday because I hadn't been asked to come in. I'd been given an involuntary holiday. I hadn't seen the bosses I worked with—the ones who didn't want me to come in. I didn't even know if they were still working in this location. They could have been in a separate area, perhaps in a separate city. I never saw them much anyway.

In the afternoon, I took a bus to pick up our daughter from day care. A tall young woman in business attire was sitting across from my daughter and me as we rode the bus home. "I hate fathers who don't work," she said.

I didn't know if she was talking to me. I had left work early but had put in my time. There could have been other fathers on the bus.

"They just stay at home all day," she continued.

"You can look me up," I said to her. "You can find out what I do."

"I've had enough of this," she said as she got off the bus.

"Look me up," I repeated.

"Don't talk to me."

I took my daughter out with me at night. I wanted her to see a friend of mine in a show. The show featured women who spoke or sang, and my friend was the MC.

My daughter and I walked to a bar called Loud Meows. At the door, a woman with a crew cut said, "You can't come in."

"Why not?" I asked.

"You have to be twenty-one."

"She's twenty-two," I said.

"How can she be twenty-two?"

"She's twenty-two months old."

"She has to stay outside."

It was cold outside; we wanted to go in.

"Can you ask the MC to come out?" I asked.

We waited, and soon my friend appeared. She was wearing a glittery sleeveless top and no coat. She was shivering. She talked to us, complimented my child, and went back inside. I wondered what was happening in there, on the small stage. Young women in sparkling clothes were probably burning the place down.

At home, I looked at my computer and saw that I'd been offered a one-time job in a different city. It was a teaching job, but I wasn't familiar with the subject. I thought I could do it and work at my office at the same time.

I emailed my boss and asked if I could work two jobs at once.

"You'll never be able to do the office job right," he said.

"I can do it," I said.

I looked through screens on my computer to find what I needed for my upcoming gig. I clicked past windows until I landed on something that looked relevant—how to design a course from the end result back to the beginning. That made sense, but could I do it for one class meeting? I was going to have to get energized. I was going to have to prepare to motivate the new students.

﹏

I took a bus to another city to get to my class. It was the cheapest bus—a round-trip ticket cost only ten dollars. The interior was comfortable, though, and the bus left on time.

I took a commuter train from the bus station to the campus. All went well during my lecture, except that one student started to cry. "You didn't see my hand when I raised it," she said. "You weren't fair to me."

"I'm sorry," I said. "Everyone gets equal time here. If I don't notice you, just say, 'Excuse me!' "

﹏

On my way back, the bus was late. I waited on the sidewalk with a number of other people. Some of them had cell phones and were making calls. I had no phone and couldn't abandon my spot. I didn't want the bus to leave without me.

The bus showed up an hour after it was scheduled.

My family didn't know where I was. But I'd saved money by taking the most unreliable bus—saving money was the important thing.

To shorten the trip, the driver pushed forward like a madman. He gunned the engine and swung the vehicle around turns. He overtook cars without hesitation. Through the window, I saw Exit signs passing in flashes.

Finding Our Way

I WAS IN A STRANGE PLACE WITH MY FAMILY—A NEW country, or a new part of our own country. Our daughter was bigger than a toddler but small enough to find happiness in minor things. We were spending time in a park before we had to leave. It was a boys' park, because it had trees for boys to climb. That is, only boys were allowed in the trees. Our daughter nevertheless had good arm strength. She could pull herself onto a horizontal branch and sit without her feet touching anything. All I could do was jump up, catch the branch with my fingers, and hang there for a few seconds before dropping off.

"Do you like this park?" I asked her.

"It's not a park; it's a garden," she said.

I looked around and noticed the large, lush trees lining the paths and, between the trees, a carpet of grass.

"It's more of a garden than a park," my wife said.

Our daughter bounced up and down. She still was not allowed to climb the trees, even though there were no boys around.

~

We saw a bulletin board that listed free activities in the city around the park. There was a hip-hop event, a comic-book conference, and an astronomy workshop (on the highest hill). But we wouldn't have time to do any of those things. We had a travel schedule and couldn't leave the place yet, but we couldn't do anything that involved a lot of time. We had to find something of interest in the park, where there were no other children.

—

I picked up my daughter by hooking my elbows around her knees and lifting her onto my back. She was almost too heavy, but she had asked me to carry her. She extended her arms to see how high she could reach. She grabbed some low-hanging branches and released them.

"Go right," she said, and I turned.

"Go left."

I followed her instructions but could feel strength draining from my muscles. My elbows wouldn't stay bent, and my knees wouldn't stay straight. We had a long way to walk—over a bridge, along a road—to get out of the garden called a park. There were markers—stones painted white—to show us the path. When we got to a significant place, we would see a name etched into a boulder.

"I'm getting tired," I said. "I'll have to put you down."

I bent my knees so she could hop to the ground. She slid a leg over my head and found her footing immediately.

—

The three of us held hands as we walked on a stone path. We didn't often hold hands, but we did now. This way, no one would get lost.

We were walking from a shaded space to a brighter, open area. An archway stood over the path that led from one side to the other.

On our side of the archway were trees and shadow; on the other were trees that opened into a clearing, through which a paved walkway passed. We might not have been going far at all. We might have been heading for the avenue that bordered the park, and from there to our destination.

As we approached the end of our walk, a man started to play a harmonica. I wasn't sure if he knew how to play the instrument. The reedy squawks didn't come together in a recognizable melody. The sounds were mostly noise; perhaps they were "art music." Still, I was glad for the familiar sounds.

The rattle of glass objects came from another direction. I pictured a bottle collector sorting through the trash. The collector would have to dig deep to find items that were worth something.

Our destination was marked with a boulder engraved with a name. I could see the end of the path but couldn't read the name yet. I was sure it said something that would tell us where we were, something that would tell us we had arrived.

Unrestful Nights

OUR DAUGHTER CALLED ME TO HER DARKENED ROOM. I climbed the loft ladder and sat on the top rung, on the edge of her bed.

"Tell me a boring story," she said.

"I bought coffee today," I said. "The counterwoman automatically gave me the sale brand. She knows I always get the cheapest kind. Today, it was mocha java. Then I caught a bus home. The driver tried to keep me off the bus by saying, 'I'm only going to Houston Street,' but that was fine with me because we live on Houston Street."

My story was not boring enough. She looked at her clock, which read "11:33."

"I'll never get to sleep!" she said. "This is the worst day of my life."

I went to her mother, who was in bed, and said, "She needs you; she's freaking out."

She climbed to our daughter's bed and came back a few minutes later.

"Is she asleep?" I asked.

"No, but she is calmer."

Her mother and I tried to sleep in our own loft bed, but after a few minutes I heard footsteps approaching. Soon, our daughter's head appeared above the edge of our mattress. "Can I sleep here?" she asked. "I won't take much room. I just need a corner."

"No," I said, but she crawled over us anyway and settled in a narrow area next to the wall.

"I can't sleep here," I said. "Three people are too many in the bed."

Truth be told, I didn't the think the bed was strong enough to hold the three of us. I had assembled the frame, and I didn't think it was solid. It was made out of relatively thin sticks of wood.

I took a blanket and a pillow and proceeded to the couch. My feet didn't fit on the cushions because the couch was too short. I lay there in the dark for a while and realized I was not going to fall asleep. It wasn't the worst day, or night, of my life, but it was close.

           —

She often stayed awake late; she was a hyperactive child. So I tried to hypnotize her to calm her down, using a method I'd seen on television. I had taken no classes in psychology. I was no doctor. I just fluttered my fingers in front of her face and chanted, "Your eyelids are getting heavy. You're feeling sleepy. You're asleep!"

I should have had a pocket watch on a gold chain to swing like a pendulum in front of her face, but I didn't have one.

On television, subjects receiving such suggestions would drop into unconsciousness. In their sleep state, they could be made to do things against their will, such as lie between two chairs like a board. Once they were there, between the chairs, you could sit on them or jump on them, and they would not bend.

I didn't want to paralyze my daughter or petrify her; I just wanted to put her into a peaceful state of slumber. I kept up my chant, my relaxing mantra, but she just looked at me. She met my eyes with her eyes. She didn't waver, and she didn't go under. When she saw my fingers fluttering in front of her face, she slapped my hand away.

—

I took out a telescope and aimed it at the moon. The sky was dark and clear, but the telescope wasn't strong. It magnified up to sixty times. When I looked through the eyepiece, I could see craters on the lunar surface.

I invited my wife and daughter to take a look. My wife crouched and placed an eye to the back lens. "There are craters everywhere," she said.

Our daughter was afraid to look. "I don't want to," she said.

"Why not?" I asked.

"I don't know what I'll see."

She wouldn't describe what she was afraid of, but I could guess. She would see moon monsters: creatures with rubbery appendages and pads on the ends of their fingers. Creatures without noses, because there was no air to breathe. Their skin would be blue, and their heads would have antennae. They would be smaller than people—about three feet tall. And there would be many of them. They would be running around the moonscape like rodents.

I looked through the telescope again and scanned the light and dark areas—the mountains and basins—for moon creatures. Was that one, skittering behind a rock? Was that a small army of them, preparing to take over a dry sea? I couldn't tell—the image of the moon wasn't detailed enough.

"It's OK," I said to our daughter. "You can look."

She reluctantly peered through the eyepiece, but I didn't know what she saw. Whatever it was, it must not have been very scary, because she didn't pull away.

—

She asked me to check her closet, to see if anyone was hiding there.

"Where would someone be hiding?" I asked. "There's no space in your closet."

"Behind the clothes," she said.

"How would someone get in there?" I asked.

"From the fire escape, through the gate."

"Do I have to check?"

"You have to. Otherwise, I can't sleep in my bed."

I opened the closet door. I saw many clothes hanging from a rod, boxes on the floor, more boxes on a shelf above the clothes. "There's no one here," I said.

"Look behind the clothes," she said.

I put my hand between the hanging dresses. I was starting to get a little frightened myself. I pushed the fabric aside and saw only darkness. "There's no one," I said, but I wasn't one hundred percent sure. I walked over to the window and looked at the gate to the fire escape. I turned the knob to see if it was latched. I pulled on the bars. The gate didn't budge. I looked through the window, but the darkness was too complete for me to make out anything. A prowler might have been staring me in the face, and I wouldn't have been able to tell.

I remembered a horror movie I'd seen when I was in high school. In the film, a woman was thought to have died, but she hadn't really died. She just looked like she had died, and so she was entombed in the basement of a mansion. Later, she showed up alive, but she looked much the worse for being buried. At that point, the whole mansion collapsed into a pit.

As a teenager, trying to sleep, I was afraid that the dead/ alive woman, or a woman like her, would show up outside my bedroom door. I wanted to go to my parents' room and sleep in their bed, but I knew that wasn't an option.

"Well, you can sleep with us tonight," I said.

I didn't mean with her mother and me. I meant she could sleep on cushions on the floor, next to us. It wouldn't be comfortable, but it might be less scary, and it was the best I could offer.

—

At night, something fell onto the floor and made a *clink* as it hit. It was something small, and the sound was not as loud as a spring-loaded mousetrap going off. I hadn't set a mousetrap, anyway. After the *clink*, I became aware of our daughter's voice from her bed in the next room. "I heard something," she said.

I wondered if she thought a robber had entered, picked up a fork, and dropped it. Or if she thought a ghost had lost a piece of jewelry. Both scenarios could explain the sound. Or maybe our pet turtle had gotten into something metallic, something like an empty tuna can. Turtles like to eat fish. But the turtle should have been safely in her tank, and we hadn't left any tuna cans on the floor.

My wife got up, went to our daughter's room, and came back. "Did you find out what fell?" I asked.

"No," she said, "and I'm not going to look for it now."

I didn't want to look for it, either, in the middle of the night. It was probably a small object, invisible to the tired eye.

In the morning, I didn't see anything that could have fallen. In fact, I'd forgotten that something had hit the floor during the night. I was not thinking that a spirit helped itself to a meal and dropped a fork. Or that a ghost threw dice in a game of supernatural craps. I wasn't thinking about the sound at all until my toe touched something foreign by the kitchen sink. It was a plastic clothes hook that I'd stuck to the freezer and fastened with a rubber band. I'd rigged the freezer door to keep it shut. The rubber band must have ripped the hook from its adhesive base. The hook must have shot off like a pebble in a catapult. It must have ricocheted off some surface—a wall or a cabinet—before it hit the floor with a *clink*.

Flats Fixed

B Y COINCIDENCE, I GOT TWO FLAT TIRES ON THE SAME day. I discovered the first one about fifty yards from where we lived. Just after I'd unlocked my bike and started to pedal, I felt the rumble of a wheel rim hitting the pavement. The back tire had no air—it was dead flat.

I believed my neighbor had punctured my tire because I was joking with him. He'd shown me a photo of a high-tech bike rack that could be installed in our basement. Each bike would have a halter, like a cow in a milking pen. "Look," he'd said, "the front wheels will sit right next to the wall."

"It'll happen," I'd said, "when we get a laundry room and a roof garden."

He found that funny, but he might have been angry because I wasn't taking him seriously. I was calling his proposal a pipe dream. He might have punctured my tire with a sharp tool then.

⌣

A young man at a repair shop removed a sliver of glass from the dead tire, and I realized my neighbor didn't damage my tube—I ran over something. After the repair guy replaced the tube, he said the fix would last a long time.

I got my second flat about twenty blocks from the shop. I was about halfway to where I was working, and I saw I'd have to walk my bike the rest of the way. Walking wasn't easy, because I had a sore foot. The faster I walked, the more it hurt. I walked more slowly than almost everyone around me. However, I caught up to an elderly woman who was using a cane. When I cut in front of her, she said, "Nice!"

I made it to my destination barely on time, dropped off my papers, and left the office to take care of my ailing bike. I carried it down a set of stairs from the street and over a turnstile, then rolled it into a subway car and propped it on its kickstand.

The woman sitting next to me said, "Your back tire needs air."

"It's flat," I said. "I just got it fixed today."

"Just today!"

"I'm taking it back to the shop now."

—

I was convinced the first repair job was faulty, but I'd been given no guarantee. When I thought about it, I didn't see how bike-tire work could be guaranteed. Still, I was annoyed.

"I left here and got this flat," I told the young repairman. "I didn't run over anything; it just blew."

He showed me a tiny hole in the rubber. "You hit something," he said. "A splinter or a sliver."

"Amazing!" I said. "Like getting struck by lightning!"

"Or winning the lottery."

—

A couple of weeks later, I unlocked my bike from its rack. The rack hadn't been replaced with neat stalls, as my neighbor had suggested. The bikes were mashed together. I pried mine free, lifted it, and carried it up the stairs.

I rode about fifty yards, then felt the telltale vibration of a flat tire. It was the same tire that had gone flat twice already. I was convinced there was some serious reason. Maybe the rim was defective—bent or flattened from misuse. But I couldn't have it fixed immediately because I was going out of town.

I returned the injured bike to its rack and thought about the flat tire the whole time I was away.

⁓

Back at the bike shop, I told the repairman, "The tire was fine when I parked the bike, but when I unlocked it and rode on it, I had a flat.

He removed the tube and pumped air into it. He dropped the tube over his head and wore it like a necklace. He swiveled it around like a Hula-Hoop.

"I don't hear anything," he said.

He set the tube aside and felt the tire with his fingers. "Here's something," he said as he pulled out a short piece of wire.

"The wire tip is the width of the rubber," he added. "It let air out only when you rode."

"A wire?" I asked.

"A short wire, stuck in the rubber."

⁓

A couple of days later, I experienced my fourth flat tire. It happened when I was a few blocks from a train station. I walked the short distance to the terminal with the bike at my side. One of my feet was sore; I didn't know why. It slowed me down, but I didn't miss my train.

While I was away, I planned my return to the repair shop.

⁓

I found that my regular repair shop had closed. I didn't know if the attendant had left temporarily or if the shop had gone out of business. There was no note of explanation. There was, however, a handwritten message from another customer, complaining that the work on his bike wasn't done right.

I walked to another repair shop. Since I had plenty of time, I didn't mind that my sore foot held me back.

When I arrived at the new shop and pointed at the tire, another young repairman asked, "How long have you had this bicycle?"

"About two years," I said. "I don't know how long it was used before I got it."

"You need a new tube," he said, showing me a fragment of glass on his fingertip, "and a new tire."

I got the new tube and tire with all of the money in my pocket. On my way out, I said, "Maybe I'll see you later."

"Hopefully not for a flat tire," he said.

⁓

On my ride home, I tried to avoid running over fragments of glass. However, when I looked closely, I saw that the street was littered with glass. Remnants of cars' side-view mirrors, pieces of windshields, and shards of bottles were strewn across the pavement. I swerved recklessly to find a clear path. I heard the crunch of my tires rolling over tiny blades.

I stopped at an intersection and saw a man walking toward me. He was staring at me—he wanted to say something.

"That's a badass bike," he said.

I didn't see my bicycle as "badass." It was designed for slow riding, with only one gear.

I thought the man didn't really see the bike. He saw a guy on a bike waiting at an intersection. I might have been blocking his path. He meant I was a badass. Or maybe he meant he was a badass, and he recognized all fellow badasses.

"It's bad enough for me," I said.

Night Route

IN MY WORKPLACE, I REALIZED I'D LOST MY BICYCLE.
I thought I'd parked it on the street, but I couldn't remember
where on the street. I might have locked it to a pole, the kind
that held a No Parking sign. But on which block? I would
have stored the bike close to the office, but there were several
heavily trafficked streets around the building. Or I might have
brought the bike in through the service entrance, not through
the lobby. The service entrance led to the basement, and from
there to the service elevator. But that elevator was usually out
of order. I might have brought the bike into the basement
and been blocked on my way through the maze of hallways.
Then I might have wheeled it back onto the street and left it
somewhere. I didn't have time to look for it, because I couldn't
leave the office. I'd be at work for several more hours, but the
time frame didn't matter. I didn't have to tell anyone where I
was. Those who knew me knew where I was.

I was thinking maybe I didn't ride my bicycle to work;
maybe I took the subway. Taking the subway wasn't a relaxing way to travel. When you got on the train, you needed to
look for who else was in the car. You didn't want to sit too
close to anyone. But I couldn't remember taking the subway,

or which train I took to which station. I didn't think a fare had been subtracted from my transit card, but there was no way to check unless I went to a station and put the card through an automated reader.

I looked into a conference room that resembled a classroom. I saw I was credited on a blackboard for contributing to a magazine article—my name was written on the board in chalk—but I was sure I'd made no contribution to the article. The piece contained an analysis of various companies' annual reports. I didn't see how I could have contributed to an article that focused on businesses' earnings before interest, taxes, depreciation, and amortization. But I might have edited someone else's work on the subject—that is what I usually did.

I left the office late at night. Outside, I didn't look for my bicycle. Instead, I looked for a place, a sort of house, that had an address farther along the street. But of course no place like this would have been open, when everything was shut. And anyway, why would I have needed a real place when everything was virtual? Along the street, I saw signs with words in Chinese characters, buildings with decorative lintels, windows that displayed red-paper lanterns, shops selling play swords with tassels. Soon, I came to a Chinatown supermarket, and I thought I might find something inside, some kind of unusual food. The market was open, and I entered without delay. I didn't find what I was looking for, but I saw a section of live seafood. I watched as a customer pointed to a tank and an attendant took a fish from the water with a small net. The attendant put the fish on a plastic tray and slid the tray along the row to the next man. The fish, probably a sea bass, flopped on the tray. The fish's next stop would be the sink.

I walked outside and spotted my bicycle—it was where I'd left it, at a horseshoe-shaped anchor. I could see the bike from a distance because it had fluorescent-green handlebars and a matching fork. I checked to see that both tires had air, unlocked the flimsy chain, and shoved off. There was little traffic on the streets. I came to an intersection, and a driver honked at me. I looked into his window and saw him pointing to the right. I made a gesture that I was going to the left. We flailed our arms as we waited for the other to move. The driver said something I could not hear and in frustration sped around me. I was not concerned. I was only a few blocks from home. My tires had air, and if one went flat I could walk the rest of the way.

Bad Job

AT MY JOB, NOT A DAY WENT BY WITHOUT A MISTAKE OF mine being discovered and held up as an example—a bad example.

"You have to go by the book," I was told.

I do go by the book, I wanted to say, but I didn't say that, because I didn't want to disagree. I had to respond obsequiously. "I'll go by the book from now on," I said. "I'll follow it to the letter."

But the next day, I heard, "You didn't go by the book. You neglected key elements of the book. You did the same thing you did yesterday and the day before. You can't get it right, can you?"

I had it right all along, I wanted to say, but I didn't say it, because I knew that contrariness was a futile response. So I said, "I'll get it right this time, the next time, and every time."

But the next day, I heard, "You don't understand what we are doing. You don't see that what you're doing doesn't fit with what we're doing. You have to stop what you're doing and do it the way we do it."

"May I ask a question?" I asked.

"No, you may not ask questions. You should know the answers already. Asking questions takes time. When you ask, you hold everyone up. We have work to do, and we have to do it now."

I began to arrive at the office early, before anyone else, except for the person who was on European time. She was friendly, showed me how to make coffee, but she was unaware of my difficulty with my job.

I needed as much time at my desk as I could get, so I could make things right.

I pointed out to my superiors that I was putting in more hours on the job.

"You're here physically," I was told, and I knew that meant I was not there mentally.

I wondered why I'd been hired in the first place. The chief who'd hired me had said that everyone "loved" me. Things couldn't have gotten much better than that. But things had changed, because the person who hired me was gone. The people who remained saw me differently. The chief's departure opened the way for the remaining, angry people.

I wanted to think of a song, a catchy song with suggestive lyrics. I wanted the song to take me away from the task at hand. I wanted it to take me to a bar, where I could sip from a jar. There, a woman would blow my nose, then blow my mind. But the song was quickly erased from my consciousness by the enumeration of my mistakes.

I sat farther down in my chair, then pulled myself up, then slid down again, as I focused on my computer screen and tried to think of all the things I hadn't thought of before—all the correct things—and tried to forget everything that was wrong. But my terrible sitting posture didn't help me. People came by and didn't see me. They thought I'd left the premises.

What about all the things I've done right? I wanted to ask, but I didn't ask, because asking would bring disapproval—for posing a question.

My onetime friends, I noticed, had become my enemies, or at least neutral observers. They (the observers) seemed to know that what I was doing was wrong, and they wanted no part of it. They directed their attention away from me, so as not to be caught on the side of wrongness. The woman on European time stopped helping me make coffee.

I was afraid that all of the criticism, reproach, and blame would lead to internal bleeding. Sooner or later, I would feel a dripping, and it would be blood, not some innocuous fluid, and it would be coming from my nose or an ear. The flow would quicken, gain in volume. Such bleeding might have had a curative effect in the old days, when it was thought to remove toxins, when people were "bled" to make them feel better. But I didn't want to be bled now. I would end up bloodless and dry.

What should I have done about this loss of blood, not to mention the loss of spirit? Should I have acquired an AK-47 and taken my revenge? But just mentioning an AK-47 would have been equivalent to threatening violence in the workplace. I knew about violence—I had to take an online course on how to avoid it. If someone was arguing with me, the idea would *not* be to gently nudge that person until he or she was at least three feet away. That nudging, that touching, would be an invitation to fight.

And even if I'd had a semi-automatic rifle, I'd be at a disadvantage. I'd be using a peashooter, and I was in a tank battle. In any case, I owned no guns and wasn't about to acquire one.

I had to come up with a quieter, more personal plan, one that helped my loved ones and me get on, because that's what we needed to do: get on with our lives.

Get on and move on. Do something I enjoyed doing. Simple as that.

Big Man

ICALLED HIM BIG MAN, BUT ONLY IN MY HEAD. HE WAS NOT very menacing because, while he was stout, he wore glasses. He was an important person, at least in our office. I didn't think he'd like to be called Big Man to his face.

⁓

I walked with Big Man to a work gathering. On the way, he told me about his background. "Where I grew up," he said, "my family was in the one percent."

I couldn't picture where he was from. It was somewhere in the south of Africa, but it was not South Africa. It was one of the places where the whites displaced the blacks.

"You were like a prince," I said.

"Or the king. But we might not be in the one percent here."

It didn't matter to me if Big Man was in the one percent in my country or not, because I was in the ninety-nine percent.

As we approached a bar, I said, "I'm worried about my work outside the office. It might take away from my job."

"Everybody does it," he said.

I didn't know if he meant that everyone in the office did outside work, or that everyone worried their outside work would take away from their job.

At the gathering, Big Man and I each had a beer. "I drink beer every night," he said. "I can't live without it."

I didn't say that drinking beer might make him even bigger than he already was. I was no fat shamer.

We drank separately, lost in the crowd. I enjoyed my beer—I was not often treated to drinks at work.

—

In the hallway the next day, Big Man asked about my extra work. "How is it going?" he said.

"It's going well," I said. "I have new projects coming up."

He looked disappointed by my answer, as if he'd expected me to say that I was not doing outside work anymore, that I'd given it up in favor of my day job.

—

Big Man brought me into a sort of conference room—a decrepit place, with flaking paint and a steam radiator. He said, "I'm not speaking for myself now. I'm speaking for the company."

He handed me a list of my faults, enumerated on paper.

"We are putting you on probation for a month," he continued. "If you improve by the end of the month, nothing will happen. If you don't, your employment will end.

"But I'm going to help you!" he added.

I had already started to put in more time in an effort to improve my work. After our conversation, I continued to arrive early and stay late. I wanted nothing to happen at the end of the month. Big Man, on the other hand, went on vacation.

—

When he returned, he took me back into the worn-out conference room.

"I hope you had a good trip," I said.

"Yes," he said.

"I've brought copies of my work to show you," I said, gesturing toward a sheaf of printouts.

"At this time," he said, "we have decided to terminate your employment."

"I guess you don't want to look at the work I've done."

"What you need to do now is go to the HR department and sign some papers."

I went to Human Resources, where a woman was expecting me.

As I finished signing the documents, she said, "You might want your supervisor to write a recommendation for you."

"Why would he do that?" I asked. "He just got rid of me."

She saw the humor in that.

⌣

Much later, I saw Big Man in a supermarket. I didn't know why we were there at the same time. It must have been more than a coincidence. What went over the devil's back had to come under his belly.

I wanted to fight with him. I wanted to do damage. Big Man was wearing his glasses, but that didn't deter me. I wouldn't lay off due to his weak eyesight. I reached into my pocket for a weapon, but I had none. Well, I had a nail clipper, but that was no weapon. What was I supposed to do, stab him with the nail file?

Around us, people were chuckling because they thought we are fighting over a woman. "His wife went with the other guy," an onlooker suggested.

Big Man grabbed me with his arms; it was almost a hug. He lifted me toward the ceiling.

I hated this man. Did he hate me? He looked like the man whose name I didn't use. I couldn't remember his proper name. I called him Big Man.

The Patient as Mobile Device

ONE GOOD THING ABOUT GETTING FIRED WAS THAT I received three free therapy sessions as part of my severance.

I was distraught, no doubt about it, and I wanted to use my last perk. I wanted to speak to a professional, at no charge, about my personal crisis.

At first, I had a hard time finding a therapist. Maybe the therapists I called didn't like the idea of giving free therapy sessions. Maybe they didn't want to talk with losers. But wasn't that a therapist's job, to work with losers?

I went to the only therapist who called me back. We met in her gloomy apartment, and she led me to a couch in her dark living room.

I began by describing my time at my ex-job. "I'd thought I'd be fired every day," I said, "but I stayed for a long time."

"You didn't seem to like your job very much," she said, "but you didn't do anything about it."

"I did a lot," I said. "I had a double life."

"You should celebrate that," she said, "You should be happy about all the things you did in secret. You should be glad no one found out."

She made a gesture to indicate victory, but I couldn't see her clearly in the dim light.

⁓

The next time I visited her, I said, "You criticized me for working at a job I didn't like and not doing anything about it."

"Do you think I was making a judgment?" she asked.

"Yes."

"You're right," she said. "I make judgments all the time. But the key is not to care what I think. That's how you can grow."

"What do you mean by 'grow'?"

"See this phone?" she said, indicating the cell phone on a small table by her chair.

She picked up the phone and turned it so it was facedown. "That's not growth," she said. "That's change."

I understood that the phone could not develop or evolve. Only its position could be shifted. I was like a cell phone. I could only go from being right side up to being upside down.

"Do you think I'm too old to grow?" I asked.

"You can have emotional growth until your last breath."

I wanted to keep growing until I took my last breath. I wanted to leave the world that way. I would take my last gasp and at the same time become more than an upside-down cell phone.

⁓

The third and last time I saw her, I said I liked the idea of growing at the moment I died.

"That's what I'm offering," she said.

"In three sessions?"

"Not in three sessions. You'll have to keep coming back."

"For how long?"

"Until you die, of course."

"But I don't have insurance. My coverage stopped when I was canned."

"I'll let you stop coming," she said, "but only if you give me a good reason."

"Well," I said, "I don't really have time. I have to look for work."

"That's not a good reason. The reason should be that you've achieved growth." She flipped her phone over on the small table to emphasize her point.

I pictured myself living life without psychotherapy. I might change, but I wouldn't grow. I'd be like that cell phone—on my back until someone turned me over. Then I'd be on my stomach.

I didn't want to spend the rest of my life like a mobile device. What if someone needed to make an important call, and I wasn't ready? There was only one thing I could hope for: growth when I took my last breath. When that moment came, I'd be home free.

"I'll think about it," I said, but I knew I wouldn't.

"I've enjoyed talking with you," she said, but I knew she hadn't.

She led me through her dark rooms to the exit door. I saw pieces of poorly lit furnishings—curtains, another couch, maybe a table—as I walked out.

Waste

MY BICYCLE HAD BECOME A TRASH RECEPTACLE. Someone had stuck a used napkin into a crevice on the handlebars. Someone else (or the same person) had clipped a half-empty water bottle into the rack behind the seat and left the bottle cap on the saddle.

I'd parked my bike where there were no garbage cans. Many people had walked by, looking for a place to throw their trash. Not finding a container, a few had put the refuse on the next-best thing: a bicycle. Never mind that the bike didn't resemble a waste can. The rider wasn't around. Who was to care?

Who were these hoodlums? I had no way of knowing. I removed the litter, swung onto the saddle, and rode.

⁓

While I was riding, I felt an intense nameless fear, though it wasn't really nameless. It was a common ordinary fear, the kind I felt to a lesser degree most of the time. Now, it had reached a peak and overwhelmed other emotions. It resided in the pit of my stomach. I was afraid I would have too much time to ride—too much unstructured time. I would not be called to do anything else, anything with a purpose. I would roam the streets on my bike (or, worse, stroll the streets on foot) and have nothing else to do. I would just coast along, looking for downhill stretches and avoiding ascents.

⌒

I formulated a plan. I identified alternate sources of income. The sources might be temporary, but I identified others that I could use if needed. I would have deadlines and would be able to meet them. I was keeping every possibility, every eventuality, in mind.

I was containing the fear, keeping it down. It had changed from a feeling in my stomach to a more general soreness, tenderness, or vulnerability. I was reluctant to venture into the unknown, because that could bring on more fear. But I would do it. I'd go out and see people—the most frightening activity I could imagine—and hope that the fear corrected itself.

⌒

At an intersection, a poodle tried to attack me. I knew it was a poodle by the curliness of its fur. The dog was not large; it might have been a miniature or toy poodle. Whatever its breed, it went after the leg I'd extended to keep my balance. It ran at me and snarled. I was surprised by the volume of its voice, and I could see its toy teeth. Fortunately, the dog was attached by a leash to its owner, a woman who seemed used to its behavior. The leash was an adjustable type—it resembled a spring-loaded tape measure—and the woman pressed a button to reel the dog in.

⌒

I got trapped behind a garbage truck. I couldn't ride around the truck; there was no space between it and the cars parked on the street. I could ride on the sidewalk, but that path was narrow, and pedestrians occupied it. Riding a bicycle on a sidewalk was illegal anyway.

No one was at the wheel of the garbage truck. Apparently, the driver was also a trash hauler. He had left the cab and was picking up black-plastic bags from the street to throw into the compactor. His job was not bad. No one was watching over him. If he wanted to sit on a trash bag and have a smoke, no one would stop him. He could listen to music in his cab—any genre he liked (probably country, possibly classical). He could park somewhere and take a nap, though such parking might have been against regulations. But who was to care?

As I rode, metal parts of my bike squeaked and groaned. I didn't know which pieces were grinding against each other. A pedal arm could be hitting the chain guard; an axle could be resisting the rotation of a wheel. But as long as the bike was rolling, I didn't mind the sounds.

I came to a fruit cart and leaned the bike against a fence— the bike had no kickstand.

The street vendor nodded at the machine with approval. "Good bike," he said.

"It's not good," I said.

"But it works. How long have you had it?"

"Three years," I said, remembering when I got the bike— just after my previous bike (a good one) was stolen from a street rack.

"How much did you pay?"

"A hundred dollars." I told him the name of the shop where I'd bought the bicycle and hoped he would remember it.

"A hundred is cheap."

The vendor had a car—he sat in it when rain was falling. I didn't know why he wanted a bicycle. In any case, he had given me confidence. I put my fruit in my backpack and rode away from the stand relatively fast, though I was actually going slowly. I snaked between cars, unafraid of a collision. I bobbed and wove, ducking my head and shrinking away when moving objects came too close. Pedestrians, when they saw me, ran out of my path.

—

I arrived at a place where there were mountains of garbage. The mountains seemed to go on for miles. The discarded objects were of many colors, but the overall effect was gray, with loose pieces of paper and cloth flapping in the wind. Birds circled above the hills of waste, now and then dive-bombing for edibles. Higher up in the sky were larger birds that might have preyed on the smaller birds. Feral dogs pawed over the mounds. As I got closer, I saw rats rummaging through the trash.

In one spot, there was a pile of cables and concrete—the remains of the World Trade Center, trucked in from Ground Zero. No creatures inhabited the wires and cement.

—

On my way home, I smelled smoke. Shortly, I saw a small mushroom cloud that rose between buildings on a downtown-directed avenue. I couldn't see exactly what had happened, but the fire was big. It had consumed a building.

Soon, I came to the block where I lived with my family. Almost immediately, I was inside our apartment, and I saw a covered plate that held food for me.

"I was worried about you," my wife said.

I wondered if my daughter was worried as well. I didn't have to ask her; all I had to do was look at her. She looked concerned. "A building exploded," she said.

From where we were, we could see the smoke cloud. The building had been about five stories high, with a restaurant on the ground floor. We learned later that people had loosened pipes in the basement in order to siphon gas. The building had filled with fumes; then something or someone had made a spark. A couple of people in the restaurant had died from the blast.

We were not close to where the building had stood, but we were too close.

"Get a Life"

WHILE RIDING MY BICYCLE, I SAW A MAN STEP INTO THE street in front of me. I steered around him—I didn't slow so he could pass. He saw me roll close, and when he was within earshot he said, "Get a light." Either that, or "Get a life."

I was in a hurry. I had a twenty-minute ride before I got to the bridge and began the climb. It was dark already, but my red taillight was on. I couldn't see it, but it must have been blinking in a steady strobe pattern, warning drivers to stay back.

The man couldn't have seen my taillight—he was wrong that I needed one, though I could have used a headlight. As for a life, maybe I needed to get one. Maybe I should have found a way not to have to ride my bike everywhere, in daylight and darkness, in good weather and bad. Maybe that was what this ticked-off man was trying to tell me.

I came to an intersection where the avenue forked. I wanted to go straight, but doing so would have meant cutting in front of any vehicle behind me. The traffic lights didn't work in concert here: The green showed on one side of the street before it signaled "Go" on the other side. I rolled ahead anyway, but when I reached the median, I couldn't go any farther. Traffic passed in front of me, so I ended up in the middle of the street, in a vehicle lane. A package-delivery truck pulled up beside me, and the driver yelled out his open door, "Red light, man!"

A woman rode toward me, ringing her bell. She was working her handlebar button frantically. "Get out of my way!" she yelled.

A man on a bicycle passed me from behind and headed toward the woman. When he got next to her, he reached out and said, "Wrong way!"

"Stay away from me!" she said.

Minutes later, I heard the squawk of a siren behind me, then saw the blue and red lights of a police car. I heard "Pull over" through a loudspeaker, but I didn't think the officer was talking to me—there were plenty of other vehicles on the street.

I covered about a block before the police car stopped ahead of me.

I rode around the cruiser, and it quickly gave chase. "Stop right there," the driver said through his open window.

I propped my bike against a lamppost as the officer approached. "You went through a red light," he said. "Why did you do that?"

I had no doubt I ran the light, but I didn't know why I did it. Maybe I was looking for oncoming traffic, not at the light. Maybe I was in a hurry to get home. But I didn't want to start a conversation. Any exchange might have seemed rude, and rudeness would have led to arrest, detainment, and penalty.

"I didn't realize I went through the light until you told me," I said.

"Do you have ID?" the officer asked.

I must not have responded quickly enough, because he said sharply, "ID! Ten hut!"

I stood to attention and gave him my driver's license and a card with a photo.

"Do you have two licenses? Is one of these fake?"

"No, one is not a license."

"Wait here," he said as he got back into his car.

Rain was falling as I stepped onto the sidewalk. My bike balanced against the lamppost. Cars passed the police car obediently.

I was sure I'd get a ticket, not only for running a red light, but for responding to an order too slowly. I guessed the fine would be hundreds of dollars. I could appeal, but then I would have to go to court. Which court would that be? Did the local traffic court have a bicycle division? Would the judge be on my side? The cops wouldn't change their story, and the judge might think that everything a cop said was true.

The arresting officer returned and said, "Your record is clean, so I'm letting you go."

I stopped at every red light on the route to the bridge. I had to cover about three miles before I reached the ramp. The traffic signals slowed me down, though I was still in a hurry.

On the bridge, there were no intersections. I could not be stopped for proceeding illegally. But the hill was steep. I pedaled slowly as I approached the first platform. I almost could not move forward, but I didn't stop. Near the top of the ramp someone had painted graffiti on the pavement: "Sarah^2, Marry Me," with a superscript "2." I didn't know what the "2" meant. Was this the second Sarah to receive a proposal? Or was she Sarah Squared? On the other side of the peak, sadder spray-painted words were spaced at even intervals on the pavement: "Entropy," "Self-Obsession," "Mediocrity," "Conflict," "Boredom," "Revolution."

I was coasting fast as I neared the exit, faster than the cars in their lane beside me. I squeezed the brake handles, then released them. I did not use the "death grip"—the motion that would engage the brakes at the risk of my life. The path narrowed as I came to the street. I had to get through a space in a wall and ease the wheels over a dip in the pavement. When I passed through the last obstacle, I would be more or less home.

Needles and Pins

I WAS RIDING IN A COLD RAIN, IN SLEET, AND I DIDN'T HAVE a hat with a bill or visor. I held my hand above my eyes to shield them, but I couldn't control my bicycle with only one hand. I was weaving on the street. My glasses were covered with drops. The ice particles were stinging my skin.

When I rode between buildings, I felt less wind, but when I turned onto a through street, I was hit head-on with a blast. It was difficult to make progress in the wall of air. I pedaled hard but only inched forward.

Inside my building, I couldn't see through my fogged glasses. I carried my bike down the stairs to the basement by feel, by the remembered position of my feet on the steps. The ridges in the metal stairs gave traction; my feet didn't slide out from under me.

~

In the evening, my wife saw someone she recognized on television. A middle-aged man was winning a movie award and was making a brief speech on stage.

"He was my boyfriend," she said. "He used to live a couple of blocks from here."

Our daughter took a photo of the TV screen to send to her social network. "You could have had a luxurious life," she said to her mother, "but instead you live here, with him." She pointed where I was sitting, watching.

"He's cuter," my wife said, referring to me, and I noticed that the award winner had a scraggly beard and a bald area on the top of his head. I had no such features. I had thick hair on my head but otherwise was relatively hairless.

The winner thanked his wife and family.

"Too bad he's married," our daughter said.

"I've met his wife," my wife said.

"You could have lived in Hollywood!"

I looked around and saw that our place had no glamour. Artwork by me and people I knew covered the walls; orange light shone in from the lamppost just outside a window. The sounds of tipsy people, car horns, and an occasional siren rose from the street below.

—

I wanted to get a tattoo of a devil's head on the back of my shoulder. I could see the face of the demon in my mind. The fiend had green eyes and red, ridged horns erupting from his forehead. His tongue was hanging out, as if he was panting or laughing. He had a beard and pointed ears; a tuft of hair sprouted from his scalp. He had no body—he was a disembodied head floating over an empty landscape. His shadow lay on the plain, and he had clones. Little devils floated in the air around him.

I remembered the image from a record album I owned when I was in high school. The band was from New York and consisted of classically trained musicians who played rock and roll. The devil's heads filled the album's front cover.

The tattoo would be hidden on the back of my shoulder—at least, for most of the time. If anyone wanted to see the tattoo, I could always pull down my shirt collar.

If the observer was a friend, he or she might say, "Cool!"

If the observer was my mother, she might say, "That's terrible! Why did you do that to yourself?"

⌣

Rain was still falling when I went out again on my bike.

I was rolling through an intersection when I heard a disturbance—a scuffle and a bang—and saw a sport-utility vehicle parked at the curb. A short man was standing on the sidewalk; he had a bat in his hand—a long white stick. A tall man got out of the SUV and yelled, "Don't touch my car!"

The short man replied, but I couldn't make out what he said. He approached the tall man and swung his stick. I heard the thud of contact.

Halfway down the next block, I could still hear their exclamations.

I almost hit a middle-aged woman who was crossing the street. "Watch where you're going!" she shouted.

She was in my lane. It wasn't my fault I nearly ran her down. "I didn't touch you," I called after her.

She made a sound, or she might not have been the one who made the sound. Maybe someone's pet barked. In any case, the sound didn't form itself into words. It was the sound of an animal expressing itself.

⌣

I took my daughter for a skin piercing because she was too young to get one on her own. We went to a shop she had chosen; it had a branch in New York and one in London. Our branch was located on a major avenue, and the entrance was discreetly placed upstairs. The London connection told me this was a place for high-quality piercing.

The young man who did the job had an arm covered with something black. It looked like the sleeve of a shirt, but no sleeve was covering the arm. The black area was an all-over tattoo, the result of nonstop needlework.

My daughter chose the smallest gold stud for her right nostril. The procedure was private, done behind a curtain. Was it painless? I couldn't tell. But it was quick, and when it was done, she seemed fine.

"You can't take it out for six months," the young piercer said. "Just disinfect it every morning and night. If you have any problems, come back and see me. I'm always here."

My daughter and I celebrated by going to a delicatessen and buying cookies.

—

I saw a man, wearing camouflage pants and a backpack, fiddling with a metal grate on the street. He used his hands delicately, and he had a shiny tool hanging from a beaded chain around his neck. The gadget looked like a silver box with a safety pin attached to it.

The man was flexible; he could reach the grate without kneeling. I didn't know if he was trying to retrieve metal objects, such as coins, that had fallen through. For a second, I thought he might be planting a bomb.

Another man came by and talked to him. They both looked through the grate, into the airspace above a subway line. They gently worked the silver gadget into the space. They could not have been planting a bomb. A stranger wouldn't have been helping another stranger blow things up.

—

On my bike, I stopped at a red light, and another rider stopped beside me. "How are you?" he asked.

"I'm OK," I said. "Do I know you?"

"I saw you here last Friday."

I looked at the street numbers on the lamppost signs. "It wasn't me," I said. "I wasn't here then. It must have been someone who looked like me."

"It was you. It was the same bike."

I was riding an old red bike. "Not mine," I said. "You saw someone else's bike."

"It was a red bike," my new companion said as the light changed. "Hello, neighbor!" he added as he shot ahead.

—

I was ready for my tattoo. I knew a shop where I could have one done. It was not as fancy as the place where my daughter and I had gone. This shop was small and cramped, with an entrance on a side street. Its walls were covered with colorful stencils. The choices were many: I could get words, abstract patterns, images of figures, or drawings of mythical beasts scored in my skin. But I wanted a devil's head with its tongue hanging out.

I expected to feel a scratching, maybe a prickling, from a single electric needle. Later, I might feel a stabbing from multiple needles. The pain might become bothersome after an hour in the chair. If so, I would ask the artist to finish quickly.

"You can have speed," the artist might say, "but you won't have quality."

"Take your time, then," I might reply. "I want you to do it right."

The artist would keep the needles humming.

—

I parked my bike at a railing next to the East River and walked down to the waterline. I boarded a boat with a group of people. Among the strangers, I saw a couple of people I knew, but I didn't talk to them. They were having a good time, but I was with them by accident. I didn't want to show them my tattoo.

The boat churned upriver, and when it docked, everyone headed for a bar. I didn't want to go along. I just wanted to get my bike and head home. I walked from the landing—it was about thirty blocks to where I'd started. But I couldn't find my bike. I knew the number of the street where I'd parked, but there were no numbered streets next to the river. The riverbank was just a plowed area that used to be lined with flowers. The landscape was being torn apart.

I made my best guess as to where a street might connect with my path, and I saw many bikes locked to a railing. I looked at the objects carefully, trying to locate an old red bike among the many two-wheelers. I didn't want to give up. I didn't want to go home on foot. I didn't want to admit that I couldn't remember.

Mirror Park

I WAS VERY THIRSTY. BUT I WASN'T FAR FROM WATER, OR SO I thought. I was on my bicycle, riding next to what had been the East River Park. The area once had a few water fountains but was now a wasteland. Piles of sand lay in place of flower gardens. A couple of drinking fountains still stood, but the valves were turned off. In fact, the fixtures were sealed off by wire-mesh fencing.

I rode along the edge of the construction zone and saw that a tennis court was now a parking lot for official vehicles. According to a signboard, the land in the former park would be raised by eight feet to prevent flooding. A diversity of trees and plants would be brought in. Pedestrian bridges and restrooms would be replaced. But the result was hard to imagine when the landscape was dirt.

To one side, I saw a park I hadn't seen before. I rode into it because a fence blocked my path forward. I arrived at a small baseball diamond and walked my bike between the bleachers and the ball field. I became the main attraction for the spectators as I interrupted their view of the kids playing. Could they see me, and what did they see? Just a guy on a bike, or someone not quite the same as they were, with their kids playing?

I was in a mirror of the park that had once existed, with people who used to frequent the original park. I almost ran into strollers holding toddlers. The passageways resembled a maze. On either side were rosebushes with brightly colored blossoms. I had no idea where the forking paths led. Shortly, I came to the innermost circle, occupied not by a Minotaur, but by a couple of young white guys. I could have guessed at what they were doing, what their relation to each other was. But I was anxious. I was looking for a street, any street, that would lead me out of the lush green place.

Among the alternate trees, I spotted an outbuilding, a sort of urban outhouse, that seemed to have plumbing. On an outside wall was a familiar arrangement of drinking fixtures, one higher for big people, the other lower for small people. I pushed a valve button, and water came out slowly, but surely. I didn't know if one tap was safer to drink from than the other. There was no sign saying the water had been tested. I let the water run and, straddling my bicycle seat, drank from the lower one. I counted the gulps. How much could I drink, or should I drink? Six gulps, at least. I took ten. I wasn't dying; I wasn't about to keel over. I was ready to go on.

Dinner Prep

I WAS PLANNING TO MAKE A DISH FROM RICE AND MIXED vegetables. I'd forgotten how to make something from these ingredients, but I wanted to change what I ate and become healthier. I usually was not vegetarian, but our daughter usually was, and I was cooking for all of us—wife, daughter, and myself. However, I didn't know how to get past step one: making the rice.

"How much water should I use?" I asked. "How much rice?"

"Look at the directions," I was told by my wife and daughter.

I read on the box: "Measure twice as much water as rice. Add butter. Boil, then simmer with the lid on." I apportioned the water, then the rice. I dropped in a spoonful of butter and turned on the burner, not to high heat, but to medium. I looked for a lid, but the one I selected didn't fit. Even so, it didn't fall off the pot, so I let it balance there.

I hoped the water was the only thing that would simmer. Any one of us could flip our lid—well, not my wife, she wouldn't do that. She was the calm one—my daughter and I could always talk to her in a reasonable way.

I was so wrapped up in making the rice that I ignored the mixed vegetables. I started the chopping, careful not to slice a finger. I had the idea that professional chefs had scars on their fingers from many wayward blades. I was no chef; I wanted to keep my fingers as they were: intact. I ended up with colorful piles of crudités. I oiled a pan (I used to have a wok, but it left my possession long before) and shoveled in the vegetables.

My next task was to set the table. I was tempted to lay the napkins out flat, but I knew my dinner companions wanted their napkins folded along the diagonal. There was something aesthetically pleasing about the triangular shape from a diagonal fold, something more attractive than what you'd get with a horizontal fold. Personally, I didn't see the difference: The napkins were going to be messed up anyway.

I had to jump from the table back to the sizzling mixture. I stirred the vegetables as they fried. I whisked the simmering rice (the lid had fallen off but didn't break), then returned to the vegetables. The heat was too high. I was getting charbroiled green and white pieces, when I wanted them slightly browned. I almost forgot to add the sesame seasoning and the soy.

Busy at the stove, I neglected the table. There was the matter of drinking glasses, and not just any glasses—the personal glass for each drinker. I found the correct vessels and looked for ice. I was lucky: There was ice, but not much. It was time to freeze more water. I wondered how long it would take water to solidify in our particular freezer. We had a cold icebox, but the temperature setting was probably not all the way down to Coldest. I couldn't gauge the actual setting, because I didn't know where the thermostat was located. I had not seen or touched the control knob in years, and I was not about to look for it now. I slid the ice tray in and waited. However, I could not focus on waiting for ice to freeze; that was like waiting for water to boil.

The next step was to bring the chairs to the table. Our table was too large for the space it occupied, so one chair (a rocker) had to be slid in, another chair needed to be unfolded, and a third chair had to be lifted over the back of the couch. While carrying the chair, I needed to watch for the head of my daughter, who might have been sitting on the unfolded chair. If I missed her head, I'd have to be careful not to hit the table. A sharp blow might cause the tabletop to come loose from its support, and the flap might collapse to its original, downward position, and everything on it might fall to the floor. But I carried the chair successfully, and we began our meal of rice and stir-fried vegetables.

Our daughter looked at my plate and said, "You are eating too much."

Handholding

My wife and i were walking hand in hand—a gesture that should have been easy. We'd held hands many times. However, we didn't need to hold hands to walk along; we didn't need to help each other around. But on this day, one of us expected the other to reach out a hand, and neither seemed to want to be the first to do it. I reached first, and my signal was returned.

We were walking along a wide street below our apartment, going from one corner to the next. The air was chilly, but we weren't wearing gloves. The sensation of touch was direct and pleasant. But as we walked, the attachment slowed us down. Still, we didn't let go, at least not on this one long block.

If we saw someone we knew, we would stop and say something, but we probably wouldn't continue to hold hands. That would have looked quirky. We wouldn't stand arm in arm, either, with my arm over her shoulder and hers around my waist. That would have looked lovey-dovey. But we didn't see anyone we knew, so we didn't have to decide what pose to take.

I stopped holding when I realized my pants were sliding off my waist. The crotch of the cloth was approaching my knees. "Wait a second," I said as I dropped my hand and went through the steps of tightening my belt: I opened my jacket, pulled the belt's tip through the buckle, found the prong, fit a punch hole over the prong, slid the tip through the loop, and closed my jacket. I extended my hand again, and it was taken.

When we reached an intersection, we interrupted our contact while waiting for the Walk signal. We had to pay attention, because this was a major crossing. Was traffic approaching? Were cars turning across our path? Did we hear a far-off siren screaming? Would we make it to the other side before the Walk timer ticked down to zero? Would we have to run as an orange-lit symbol warned us to stop? Would we have to cover our ears as the siren blasted in our faces? We joined hands again on the other side of the intersection.

Holding hands had meaning, but maybe the gesture had meaning only for me. That couldn't have been right. It also must have had meaning for my wife, but that meaning might have been different from the significance it had for me. In my mind, the act brought back memories of the times of not holding hands, times when I had no hand to hold. But we were trying to make those times right, to turn things around. Could it be done? My cynicism kept me back, but my hopefulness pushed me forward. We had the chance now to appreciate the holding and take the next step. We could advance to some other form of affection—for example, hugging. An arm around a neck or around the shoulders—that was the ticket! And who knew where we'd go from there? I knew. We'd go from hugging to putting on music and dancing.

Time to Check In

M Y MOTHER SAID, "DON'T COME. YOU DON'T HAVE TO visit. It's too much trouble."

And I thought, Maybe I should listen. Maybe I should not go. My presence might be stressful. She might wonder what to do for me, what to do *with* me. But I said, "I want to visit. I'm coming to visit."

"I don't cook anymore," she said. "My meals are delivered. The deliveryman used to be a musician in the local jazz orchestra."

"I'll get my own food," I said.

"OK, you can visit," she said, and I wondered if she was really looking forward to seeing me, or if she was just trying to end our conversation. Talking on the phone was hard for her, because, in those minutes, her ability to hear would fade and she would find herself speaking without hearing a reply.

"I'm hanging up now!" I yelled into the receiver.

I went to the local car rental agency and got my standard tiny car from an attendant who was my friend. In fact, we called one another "my friend." I drove through a maze of half-finished ramps and cloverleafs on the west side of the Holland Tunnel to take a "shortcut" to the main interstate route. On the highway, I went without stopping until I was out of New Jersey.

I was a little wound up from the drive, experiencing perhaps the beginnings of white-line fever. When I stopped for coffee, I spilled my hot drink on the counter next to the cash register. I was embarrassed and apologetic, thinking I had some sort of tremor disorder, but the people in the store didn't seem to hold my shakiness against me.

A few hours later, as I approached my mother's house or, rather, her building—my parents had converted a social hall into a living space—I stopped to pick up some food for myself.

As I got out of the car, I saw the young deliveryman leaving. "Hello," I said.

"Hello," he replied. "Your mother told me about you."

"What did she say?"

"She showed me a poem you wrote about a bad saxophone player. I play the saxophone."

"That wasn't you," I said.

He waved but didn't stop.

When I walked in, my mother was waiting for me, and she seemed genuinely happy to see me. I felt the same about her. I took out my food and gave her a present: two large mangos from a fancy-food store in New York.

"I'll go out for breakfast in the morning," I said.

"You don't have to," my mother said. "I have coffee, juice, bread, and eggs. But you'll have to make them yourself."

I could handle that. I knew I could. It would be a better breakfast than I usually had.

Home Visit

IN THE SUMMER, MY DAUGHTER AND I VISITED MY MOTHER. My wife didn't make the trip because she had to work. My mother suggested that we eat dinner outside, on the lawn next to her house. We joined together to bring out a small table and folding chairs. My mother didn't eat with us; she stood apart, wearing an apron.

She seemed able to understand us when we spoke, but she may have been using her eyes more than her ears.

"Where are the insects?" I asked, spreading my arms.

My mother said, "It's the DDT."

My daughter and I were still outside after the light had faded.

"I used to see bats around this time," I said.

I looked up through the spaces between trees, but all I saw were the silhouettes of branches, narrowing to leafy twigs.

"There's a bat!" my daughter said.

Sure enough, a descendant of Dracula flitted across an opening between the leaves. Then another appeared, and the two creatures circled, vanishing behind the foliage before returning to our field of vision. They made no sound; we couldn't hear their ultra screams. They were looking for the few insects that might have still existed.

⌣

I arranged for a prospective caregiver to visit my mother. When the woman arrived, my mother set a timer for one hour. My daughter didn't attend the meeting.

"Seeing people makes me nervous," my mother said.

She fetched her blood-pressure kit from a cluttered shelf to prove her point. She wrapped the cuff around her arm and turned on the gauge. The needle read 210 on the high end—a sign of hypertensive crisis.

"What happens if you need to go to the hospital?" I asked. "Who will take you?"

"I'll mow the lawn," my mother said. "Pushing the lawn mower will relax me."

"Shouldn't you take the medications your doctor prescribed?" the potential caregiver asked.

"The drugs make me sick."

When the timer rang, the prospective caregiver left. Later, I saw my mother on the edge of her lawn. She was wearing a hat against the sun and guiding a power mower across the grass.

⌣

After my daughter and I had left, my mother called to tell me the caregiver had not arrived for a scheduled visit.

"We should give her a couple of days," I said. "I'll send her a message."

The caregiver replied to my text question, saying she couldn't make the next meeting with my mother. I asked if she could schedule a visit after that, but I never heard from her again.

⌣

On the phone, my mother told me, "Everything is fine."

She went on to say that she'd heard a commotion in the vent over her stove. She didn't want an animal to come through the duct into her kitchen. She'd been able to close the vent but didn't know if the creature found its way out.

"Do you know what it was?" I asked.

"What?" she said.

"Was it a bat?"

"A cat? No, I don't think it was a cat. I heard a chirping in my ceiling."

"Was it a bird?"

"Yes, I heard it."

"A squirrel?"

"I have no quarrel with it."

"Maybe you should find your hearing aid and call me back."

"I'm fine. I'll call you tomorrow."

There wasn't much I could do, except wait for her call. I would worry about her, about her well-being, until we spoke again.

Cemetery Walk

THE PATH WAS KNOWN TO ME, SO I LED MY MOTHER AND sister along it. My sister had come from California to meet me at our mother's home. At first, the track looked like a dirt lane over a hill—up one side and down the other—leading from the house where we all used to live. We were walking because my mother was able to walk. We were taking advantage of her ability as we headed toward the cemetery.

As it turned out, my mother knew the path better than I did. She led us through the parking lot behind a church, then across a yard to the highway. I wasn't comfortable walking at the side of the macadam—I didn't feel safe. Cars traveled fast, and pets and people had been hit and killed. Still, it wasn't far to the turnoff, and our mother was doing well. She was energetic, animated, probably because she wanted to get to the cemetery quickly.

My sister was not doing too well. "I can't see where the ground goes up and down," she said. "It looks flat to me."

My mother and sister held hands, and I walked in front of them. Suddenly, I heard a sound of impact, turned, and saw they had fallen. They must have tripped on something, maybe a tree root, and had gone down together. I was afraid they had sprained or fractured bones, but they got up unharmed.

"We didn't see anything," my sister said. "One of my eyes doesn't work."

I remembered that she'd had a lazy eye since she was a child.

We took an unmarked road that led uphill. On one side was the old burial ground, and on the other was a newer area, with fresh-turned earth.

"In China," my mother said, "my family has only a marker. There's no room in the ground for graves."

I assumed we were going to the newer side—we knew people who rested there. But my sister wanted to go to the old part, where the stones were dated from the eighteen hundreds. "Let's find the grave of Keturah Candy," she said. "Our father liked her."

I saw that the occupant of that grave lived to be only sixteen.

"Our father wanted to talk to her," my sister said.

"He could talk to her," my mother said, "when he lit the right incense."

We crossed the road and found the granite marker for my father and brother. It was not large, but it was new and polished. And it had been free, given by the U.S. government for my father's military service. My father and brother were always at each other's throats, but now they shared a stone.

When my father passed, a friend sent me a sympathy card. It showed a field and sky, and in the sky the friend had painted a miniature flying saucer. A space alien sat in the cockpit. The creature had green skin, a bald head, and antennae with knobs on the ends. He was looking out of the saucer's glass dome at me.

"We can talk to all our ancestors," my mother said, "if we burn incense with black smoke."

As we walked away, a shadow crossed the ground. It must have been made by a fast-moving object between us and the sun. The object wasn't a cloud; it was moving too fast. It might have been a jet plane—we were on a flyway between cities. I looked up but saw no plane, no vapor trail.

"Did you see that?" I asked.

"All I see is a bright, white sky," my sister said.

"Let's keep looking," my mother said. "Let's look everywhere."

Acknowledgments

These pieces originally appeared as follows:

"After the Passing" in *Identity Theory*

"At the Writers' House" in *Flora Fiction*

"Bad Chemistry" in *The Westchester Review*

"Big Man" in *The Blue Nib*

"Bird-Watching" in *Toasted Cheese*

"Bun Dong" in *Blended Future Project*

"Bus Rides" in *The Harpoon Review*

"Cat's Teeth" in *Copper Nickel*

"Cemetery Walk" in *FRiGG*

"Changeups" in *Constellations*

"Class Walk" in *Corvus Review*

"Coked Up" in *Bad Pony*

"Days of Rain" in *K'in*

"Dinner Prep" in *FRiGG*

"Finding Our Way" in *Middle House Review*

"Flats Fixed" in *The Doctor T. J. Eckleburg Review*

"'Get a Life'" in *Posit*

"Hellfire" in *In Honour of the Artist*
(anthology, Dreammee Little City, London-Orlando)

"Holding the Gun" in *Wilderness House Literary Review*

"Home Visit" in *Random Sample Review*

"Iced" in *300 Days of Sun* and *Winter's Vindication*
(anthology, SummerStorm Press)

"Into the Box" in *A Gathering of the Tribes*

"Island Visit" in *Cosmonauts Avenue*

"'It's Here!'" in *THAT Literary Review*

"Lampblack" in *Carousel*

"Lines and Maps" in *Local Knowledge*

"Making Plays" in *The Broadkill Review*

"Meeting the Train" in *Rabid Oak*

"Mirror Park" in *Fictive Dream*

"Needles and Pins" in *Unlikely Stories*

"New Age" in *Two Hawks Quarterly*

"Night Route" in *Fictive Dream*

"Not a Pass," in *Mortal* magazine.

"Nowhere Boy" in *Indicia* and *Schuylkill Valley Journal*

"The Patient as Mobile Device" in
Flash Fiction Magazine and *Schuylkill Valley Journal*

"Police Truck" in *Festival of Language*

"Push-Button Knife" in *The Chaffin Journal*

"Questionable Moves" in *The Bookends Review*

"Safe Colors" in *Newfound*

"Seeing the Light" in *Track//Four* and *Skid Row Penthouse*

"Sights and Sounds" in *Ghost City Review*

"Strangers in the Night" in *Live Encounters*

"Through the Air" in *Pine Hills Review*

"Time to Check In" in *Fictive Dream*

"To the Maxx" in *Fictive Dream*

"Unrestful Nights" (excerpts) in *FRiGG* and *Matter Press*

"Unworldly Incidents" in *Little Patuxent Review*

"Waste" in *Boog City*

*

"Bird-Watching" was an editor's pick in *Toasted Cheese*.

"Finding Our Way" was a finalist for
Middle House Review's editor's choice award.

"Home Visit" was nominated for Best of the Net.

"Not a Pass" was a finalist in
Mortal magazine's short-essay contest.

"Nowhere Boy" was nominated for
Best of the Net and the Pushcart Prize.

*

I'D LIKE TO THANK Randi Hoffman and Nava Renek for reading the manuscript,
and The Betsy Hotel in South Beach, Miami, for providing a residency.

THADDEUS RUTKOWSKI grew up in central
Pennsylvania and is a graduate of Cornell
University and the Johns Hopkins University. He
is the author of seven previous books of prose
and poetry. His novel *Haywire* won the Asian
American Writers' Workshop's members' choice
award, and his memoir *Guess and Check* won an
Electronic Literature award for multicultural
fiction. He teaches at Medgar Evers College
and received a fiction writing fellowship from
the New York Foundation for the Arts. He has
been a resident writer at Yaddo, MacDowell and
other colonies, and has been a sponsored reader
in Berlin, Hong Kong and Singapore. He lives
with his wife in Manhattan.